Praise for *Iced in Paradise*

"A delicious multicultural mystery with an instantly lovable heroine, lively family dynamics, and a vivid sense of place. I inhaled it like my favorite shave (not shaved!) ice!"
—Sarah Kuhn, author of *Heroine Complex*

"*Iced in Paradise* proves why Edgar-winning author Naomi Hirahara is among today's best traditional mystery writers. She magically intersperses Hawaiian culture with an intriguing murder mystery. It's a good thing this is a planned series because you'll want to spend lots of time with Leilani Santiago and in her family's shave ice store. The next best thing to actually going to Hawai'i."
—Kellye Garrett, Agatha, Anthony, and Lefty award-winning author of *Hollywood Homicide*

"I tore through this book, delighting in the authenticity of the setting as much as the nuanced cast of characters. Naomi Hirahara has once again crafted a complex mystery steeped in culture that readers will adore."
—Jill Orr, author of *The Good Byline* and *The Ugly Truth*

"Hirahara depicts local flavors and a gorgeous setting few Mainlanders ever see, along with the challenges of life on a tourist-driven island. This is a delightful new series that promises more compelling adventures of this sharp-witted, relatable heroine."
—Cynthia Chow, branch manager of Kaneohe Public Library, O'ahu

Praise for Naomi Hirahara's Mysteries

"A shrewd sense of character and a formidable narrative engine."   —*Chicago Tribune*

"Hirahara's well-plotted, wholesome whodunit offers a unique look at LA's Japanese-American community, with enough twists and local flavor to keep you guessing till the end."   —*Entertainment Weekly*

"A thoughtful and highly entertaining read."   —*Library Journal* (starred review)

"Hirahara has a keen eye for the telling detail and an assured sense of character."   —*Los Angeles Times*

"This perfectly balanced gem deserves a wide readership."   —*Publishers Weekly*

"What makes [the *Mas Arai*] series unique is its flawed and honorable protagonist...a fascinating insight into a complex and admirable man."   —*Booklist* (starred review)

"Hirahara's complex and compassionate portrait of a contemporary American subculture enhances her mystery, and vice versa."   —*Kirkus Reviews*

"In author Hirahara's deft hands (she's an Edgar winner), the human characters, especially Mas, always make for a compelling read."   —*Mystery Scene*

Iced in Paradise

A Leilani Santiago Hawai'i Mystery

Naomi Hirahara

PROSPECT
· PARK ·
BOOKS

Published by Prospect Park Books
2359 Lincoln Avenue
Altadena, California 91001
prospectparkbooks.com

Distributed by Consortium Book Sales & Distribution
cbsd.com

Library of Congress Cataloging-in-Publication Data

Names: Hirahara, Naomi, 1962- author.
Title: Iced in paradise: a Leilani Santiago Hawaiʻi mystery / Naomi Hirahara.
Description: Altadena, California : Prospect Park Books, [2019]
Identifiers: LCCN 2019002885 (print) | LCCN 2019005666 (ebook) | ISBN 9781945551604 (Ebook) | ISBN 9781945551598 (paperback) | ISBN 9781945551635 (hardback)
Subjects: | GSAFD: Mystery fiction.
Classification: LCC PS3608.I76 (ebook) | LCC PS3608.I76 I28 2019 (print) | DDC 813/.6--dc23
LC record available at https://lccn.loc.gov/2019002885

Cover illustration by Edwin Ushiro
Cover design by Susan Olinsky
Interior design by Amy Inouye, Future Studio
Printed in Canada

For Rowan

In Hawai'i we say shave ice.
If you say shaved ice,
we know that you're not from around here.

—A sign on the wall of Santiago Shave Ice on Kaua'i

Chapter One

"Rainbow, Blue Monster, Waimea Wonder—" I call out from behind the counter. Even though it's about eighty degrees outside, balmy with a slight spring breeze, my fingers are frozen through my plastic gloves from guiding a block of ice through our $2,000 shave ice machine. I stand in my orange Crocs on a slated wooden platform, a creation of our ever dependable friend, Darrell, whom everyone calls D-man. D-man is like my second father, or sometimes more my father than my real dad. At least D-man's usually around my family, while my own father is like a magician—here one moment and gone when you're not looking.

A family of redheads steps forward to receive their shave ice. They're Mainlanders, probably from a place where the sun don't shine. The boy, who looks about twelve, has a mean sunburn on his cheeks and shoulders. He's shirtless, just in his swimming trunks and rubbah slippahs. In other words, perfectly dressed for our little Hawaiian garden isle of Kaua'i.

It doesn't surprise me that the boy claims the plastic bowl with the Rainbow ice. A stripe each of blue Hawaiian, cherry, and banana. It's eye-catching, typical, safe, perfect for a boy who can't yet grow whiskers. The father takes his Blue Monster, my sister Sophie's creation. Blueberry, root beer, and chocolate ice cream, topped with mochi bits, a disgusting concoction. I'm always surprised when anyone orders it. And then there's the Waimea Wonder, my grandmother's signature combination.

"What is that brown stuff?" The mother frowns.

"Azuki. Japanese red beans. Comes in Waimea Wonder." *Dang, lady, can't you read our chalkboard?* In perfect script in multicolored chalk, complete with little flowers and hearts instead of dots for the i's, my youngest sister, Dani, has clearly written: "Waimea Wonder: haupia and pineapple with snowcap (condensed milk) and azuki beans."

"I told her no beans." She gestures to the figure looming in the corner on a stool beside me.

My grandmother, who is perched by our original 1970s cash register (I've been trying to get her to use a Square instead, but she says, "No can"), pretends that she doesn't hear the woman.

"Eh, sorry, ma'am," I apologize and take the Waimea Wonder from her.

I quickly shave her a new one, pouring haupia and pineapple syrup from glass bottles, patting it down, and shaving more ice on top. I squeeze the condensed milk from a plastic bottle—the perfect snow top.

I present it to her in a pink plastic bowl, hoping the neon color will pacify her. She doesn't seem that pleased, but I notice that she starts slurping it down immediately, not even waiting to sit down with her family at the picnic table outside.

"Baachan, you wen hear her right."

"May-be," she says.

Baachan don't play, especially with anyone who messes with her Waimea Wonder and its azuki beans.

Let me just say that it hasn't been easy moving back to Waimea from Seattle. I came home a couple of months ago, mostly for Mom, but I don't let her know that. I tell everyone that I need a break from the rat race in Seattle, that I'm missing the sun and I think that I'm coming down with SAD, seasonal affective disorder. But the truth is, I love the rain and gray skies. I love that Seattle seems angry and depressed for most of the year. That its Pioneer Square is built atop an older city and that you can even traipse through the Underground. There are layers to Seattle, while on Kaua'i, what you see is usually what you get.

Nothing seems to have changed in my hometown since my high school years. Our sign, "Santiago Shave Ice," which my Grandpop Santiago painted on driftwood almost fifty years ago, is still outside the shop. As long as I can remember, there's only been this half-block stretch of businesses we call Waimea Junction along the highway. The individual stores have changed hands a bit—Auntie Lulu's sadly is no more, and I miss the smell of chocolate chips baking in her macadamia cookies.

This southwestern side of the island is less lush than the north. Our beach along the bay is still and shallow—fewer surfers and tourists here. But we aren't far from Pakala Beach, with its Infinities surf break, which literally feels like it goes on forever—at least that's what my dad and his local friends think. We are at the foot of the road to get to Waimea Canyon, our island's Grand Canyon. Most of our customers, in fact, are covered in a reddish dust following their strenuous hike up the road. After that trek, they are ready for fluffy and syrupy sweet iced goodness.

My BFF, Court, comes through the open door carrying one of her beautiful floral creations. "I brought this for your dad," she says. It's a lei made of tuberoses and ti leaves, and the fragrance of the white waxy flowers is intoxicating, filling our little shack with organic perfume.

"So pretty," I say. Court inherited her adoptive mother's artistry, and although there are plenty of flower shops on the north side of Kaua'i, some folks come all the way to Lee's Leis and Flowers, next door, to order their wedding floral arrangements.

"Oh, Tutu Annabelle, you lookin' good," Court says. It's always strange to hear someone say my grandmother's first name, because it sounds so old-fashioned and formal. And until Court mentions it, I hadn't noticed that Baachan had cleaned up for my father's special appearance today. She's wearing a new, unstained housedress. She even took a comb to her salt and pepper hair, which she ties back with a thick rubber band that used to be around stalks of broccoli.

"You always look good," Baachan says to Court. She gestures toward me. "Not like some people."

"Whatchu tryin' for say, Baachan?" My frizzy hair is held back in a bun with a pencil. Maybe I slept in the purple T-shirt I'm wearing, University of Washington, with our husky mascot. "Eh, I took a shower before I put this on," I tell her.

As Baachan and I go back and forth, Court silently coils the lei into a clear clamshell and places it on the counter.

"You give um him yourself," I tell her.

"No, you."

I know what Court is up to. She is such a peacemaker. She knows that things haven't gone that smoothly between me and my dad in the past. A tuberose lei is a perfect diplomatic offering.

My mother enters to pick up Baachan, whose four-hour shift is close to ending. She wears her hair pretty much how she's worn it for probably the past forty years—bangs with the rest cut blunt at her shoulders—except now, instead of shiny blond, the strands are half gray and frizzy.

"Hello, Auntie. Betcha happy Uncle coming home," Court says.

Mom smiles. Today is a good day for her. She woke up early and even put on some makeup. Most of the time, she doesn't bother. It usually melts off by the afternoon.

"Leilani helped make this for him." Court holds up the packaged lei for Mom to see.

Such a liar, I think. But I accept it anyway. It will make Mom happy to think that I was thinking of Dad. I have been thinking of him, actually. Thinking about every broken promise.

My two younger sisters, both wearing backpacks, barge in from Saturday Japanese-language school. Fourteen-year-old Sophie, wearing a Black Butler manga T-shirt, is first. Of the four of us, Sophie looks the most Japanese. I have more Filipino features, and the youngest, Dani, and Emily, who is a first-year law student at Santa Clara University in California, both have wavy blond hair. Let me just say that we confuse strangers when we all go out to a family dinner—more on the Mainland than Hawai'i, however.

"Somebody wen order a Blue Monster today," Baachan says to Sophie, who lifts her skinny arms in triumph. She goes to a small chalkboard that she has nailed to the wall and with a nub of chalk adds another hash mark to seven already on the board.

"See, Leilani, Blue Monster gettin' popular."

"I don't think eight orders make anyting popular."

"Well, you haven't come up with your signature ice."

Sophie was right. Even Emily has her Ice Princess combination—coconut snowcap with vanilla ice cream—on the board.

"Well, she's back and she will," Mom says. For a moment, she seems like the old Mom, the Mom before the diagnosis. Wendy Ellis Santiago, former star volleyball setter with killer multitasking skills, handy in raising us four girls.

"Howzit, everyone—" Our part-timer, Sammie, appears, only five minutes late. She attends the community college and always claims that her studies affect her punctuality. But we all know the truth—that it's usually drama involving a guy. She scans our family's faces. "So what I wen miss?"

There's a lull in the late afternoon—March is definitely not our busy season—and I sit outside on our picnic table, itching for a cigarette. I started smoking in Seattle and I've been trying to quit. Since being diagnosed with multiple sclerosis, Mom has been kind of a health nut. She's gone paleo and lost a ton of weight. She's skinnier than me, but then that's not saying much. I've always been big boned, taking after my Filipino side rather than my Japanese or haole, white, ancestors. People, in fact, say that I'm the spitting image of my Grandpop Santiago, which, based on his beer belly in the photos around the shop, is not a compliment. I notice that both of us have big boobs.

Smoking is how I met Travis, outside our office building in a Seattle suburb. He looked like any other analyst at our company, but there was something about his eyes. They looked gray under cloudy skies and a silver blue in the sun. When he spoke to me, he looked straight into my face, as if he really wanted to hear what I was saying. Soon after we moved in together, Travis announced that he was quitting smoking, as if that had been only a ploy for him to get to know me. I told him that I would too. I lied.

We are doing that long-distance thing. You know, the thing that rarely works. I tried to do it with my old high school boyfriend, Kūheakapu Kahuakai (everyone who is not native Hawaiian just calls him Kelly). Kelly was a buddy before we got romantic. That was around the time he became born again, so we never really "did it," though we did practically everything except that. At UW, I fell hard for my resident adviser in my dorm, and soon Kelly became a distant memory. When I suggested that we break it off, he didn't put up a fight, probably because he was already falling for Court.

My cell phone dings and I position it away from the sun so I can see the screen. It's a text from Emily:

Dad there yet?

I type, *No. Are u surprised?*

Be nice.

Im always nice

She sends me that laughing emoji before she goes to work at the college library. Emily is the book-smart one, compared with me, who dropped out of UW after three years. My sister, in contrast, is a bookworm and wants to be an international lawyer. Emily is the favored child of both my parents, but I don't mind. I would pick her over me any day.

I pull out a flattened cigarette pack from my fanny

pack. Inside is one cigarette, my allocation for the day. I tap the pack against my wrist and pull out the sole cigarette. A Bic lighter, and I'm in business.

"Those things killers. They kill your grandfather." I hear that familiar, gruff voice.

I turn to see my father pulling his suitcase over some red dirt. Behind him, getting out of the taxi SUV, is the driver, Mama Liu, who could be anywhere from fifty to seventy. Her shoulder-length hair is almost all gray and her face leathery and dark from years of being out in the sun. It's a wonder that she can see the road with her drooping eyelids.

"Dad." I drop my cigarette onto the ground and smash it with my Croc.

My dad, a few gray hairs in his brown goatee, is wearing an unbuttoned Hawaiian shirt over his tank top. But instead of hibiscus flowers, the shirt features various surf sayings in graffiti style: hang ten, gnarly, stoked, and so on. My dad is trying to be cool. Urban. Instead, he looks ridiculous. I recognize the logo by the front pocket. It's a giant wave and then the writing "Killer Wave." This is my father's brand, which he has expanded into clothing. Getting out of the other side of the SUV is a young haole man, wearing the same shirt, only his is blue instead of black. He's my dad's surfing protégé, Luke Hightower.

"Luke, my oldest, Leilani."

"Hey," Luke greets me. He has crispy blond hair and a spray of freckles on his cheeks. The hairs on his arms and legs are golden against his tanned skin. He looks like a typical California surfer, so it doesn't surprise me when he reveals that he's from the OC.

"Like my mom. She's from Fullerton."

Judging from their matching outfits, Luke apparently has become my father's surrogate son. My dad always wanted a boy. Dani, Santiago Sister No. 4, was his last chance. She was supposed to be a Daniel, but I don't tell her that. I was already sixteen when she was born, old enough to hear and understand my father's disappointment. That's why I refused to pick up my father's sport, surfing, and went for my mother's, volleyball, instead.

While I've always tried to swim in a different direction than my father, Sophie has been the opposite. She's like a stray puppy, always chasing him for his approval. It doesn't surprise me when she appears outside. She can smell him a mile away.

"Daddy!" She runs toward him and wraps her arms around his neck. Dani is only a few steps in back of them and jumps on his back.

"Did you see Mom?" I ask. It's a trick question, because I know he hasn't been by the house yet.

"I will. Luke and I just have a few things to go over. We have our competition tomorrow."

You would think that the first thing you would want to do after being away from home for a couple of months is to see your sick wife. But not the king of surf.

Despite Mama Liu not being even five feet tall, she starts to unload a couple of surfboards in black travel bags and a rollaway sporting the British flag from the back of her jeep.

"You girls help," Dad tells us. "Put all dis in back of Killer Wave and start cleaning our sticks. And go get yourself shave ice, Luke. It'll be on me. Meet me at the bar on da oddah side."

I roll my eyes as Sophie practically jumps to it and

awkwardly lifts both surfboard travel bags by their cloth
handles. Mama Liu waves goodbye and drives off, her
wheels spitting back a few red pebbles.

"You can help, too, Leilani," Dad says.

Can't they be responsible for their own damn luggage? I
think as I take hold of Dad's roller suitcase. Dani claims the
boy's Union Jack one.

"Nice shirt," I say, my voice dripping with sarcasm.

"Leilani," my father warns. This clothing line has been
his baby for the past two years.

As Luke heads for Santiago's, we Santiago girls push
our way into Killer Wave. This surf and snorkel rental shop
is officially my dad's, but now Kelly manages it. He used to
have dreams, just like I did. He wanted to leave the Islands
and major in international business. He actually could have
gone to at least a four-year UH program on O'ahu, Maui,
or the Big Island, but he, like Court, never made it out of
Kaua'i.

Kelly comes out from the back, wiping his hands with
a rag.

"The King's here," I announce Dad's arrival.

Kelly smiles, but then he almost always does. That's one
of the more maddening parts of his personality, but also
the best part of it, too. When we were together, Baachan
called us Sweet and Sour. You can guess who was the sour
one. Now that he's with Court, Baachan calls them Double
Sweet. Kelly's older brother, Pekelo, on the other hand, is
more like me. In the past he seemed to carry a torch for my
sister Emily, who's more on the quiet, observant side. When
she speaks, we all listen.

Kelly tries to take the surfboards from Sophie, but she
resists. "Dad says we should start cleaning them," she tells

him as she and Dani take the boards and luggage to the
back room.

"Let her do it. Dat's da closest she'll get to Dad."

"You dark, eh."

"Well, guess where he is now." I gesture toward my left.
After retiring from being a lifeguard for thirty-five years,
D-man took over the small bar at the end of our little shop-
ping area. The bar is literally only six feet long; he actually
uses an old distressed surfboard as the main surface. When
it gets busy, people spill into the street, which raises the ire
of our local police sergeant, Dennis Toma, who apparently
is related to our relatives on the Mainland. That connection
hasn't bought us any love, especially for me and my dad.

"I thought he stopped drinking."

"Yah, well we know how that goes."

Luke walks past Killer Wave with his shave ice.

"Dat's da new prince."

"Oh, Luke Hightower?" Kelly heads toward the open
door to get a better look.

"You've heard of him?"

"Seen him surfing on YouTube. He can shred." Kelly
walks back to the counter and picks up his phone. For the
next twenty minutes, we are checking out YouTube videos
featuring Luke Hightower slicing through waves in Australia, Tahiti, his hometown of San Clemente, and here in
Hawai'i. Kelly wasn't kidding. The California boy is good.

"Nice he come help Kaua'i," Kelly says. "Lotta folks
will come out to see him."

I grudgingly agree. This competition is more of a
fundraiser than anything else to help people, especially on
the North Shore, financially recover from the devastating
floods of a year ago. My father was spearheading the event,

recruiting a handful of high-profile surfers, including Luke, to participate.

As I swipe the screen to watch another video, I hear a familiar bellowing voice coming out from D-man's place.

"I go. You stay," I tell Kelly. "Just keep my sisters away." While in high school, I had cleaned up enough of my dad's drunken escapades. It was the day after my high school graduation that we really had it out. He had done his disappearing act again, and the whole fam—Mom, Emily, Sophie, and even Dani—was out looking for him during my graduation ceremony. Only D-man and Baachan were there for me, and even she was murmuring under her breath, "No good baka buggah," about her missing son. Of course, he was eventually found, in the middle of some taro fields, soaked in tequila and butt naked.

As I run to D-man's, my father's yelling, "After all this time and money I've invested in you. And you go and stab me in the back." There's a young haole couple, perhaps honeymooners, also at the bar, looking a bit stunned.

When my father sees me, he curses, gets on our communal scooter, and putt-putts away.

"D-man, you have to stop him," I say.

"He's not drunk. Just pissed off. He'll cool off." He accepts some money from the newlyweds, who seem in a hurry to leave.

"What happened?"

Luke looks sick to his stomach. "I told him that I accepted a sponsorship from a new clothing company from Australia."

"But what about Killer Wave—" I say. I'm not a fan of my dad and his shirts, but I know that he's invested so much in his brand. And he probably was counting on his rising-star pupil to help make a big splash in the surf world. I don't know much about the business, but I'm pretty sure two clothing sponsorships is one too many.

"I hope he can forgive me," Luke says.

I glance over at D-man, who's wiping some spilled liquid from the bar. Even though he's wearing sunglasses as usual, I can tell we are on the same wavelength. It's like those old Japanese samurai movies that Baachan loves to watch on the KIKU TV. Dad never forgives. And neither do I.

Chapter Two

LUKE IS VISIBLY UPSET. Kelly has apparently been unable to hold back my sisters any longer; they have come running to see what the excitement is all about. I tell Sophie to take the surf prince over to our house. We live just a couple of blocks up the hill, so they can walk.

"Where's Dad?" Sophie demands.

"He had to run some errands," I lie.

"It sounded like he was yelling."

"Nah, he just playin' around," D-man responds, his bar counter now freshly cleaned off.

"You probably hungry," I say to Luke. Rainbow shave ice can sustain a pro surfer for only so long.

"I'm supposed to meet my girlfriend at Bamboo Royal. That's where a group of us are staying."

Bamboo Royal is a high-end bed and breakfast in Moloaʻa, below a forest reserve, on the way to Hanalei Bay. I've only gone there once, when I was helping Court with a wedding flower delivery last summer. Judging from the light, it's around six o'clock, still in the middle of rush hour. Plus, it's a Friday. If I were to give him a ride now, it would take me an hour and a half to get there and then another hour to come home.

"Well, at least eat beforehand," I say, more for my benefit than his.

"C'mon," Dani says to him. "We just up the street."

I know that Mom's been cooking Dad's favorites. Pancit, lumpia, and chicken adobo. I hope that OC boy can hang with Filipino food.

Sophie reluctantly follows those two across the empty highway. She can sense that I'm lying about our father, but she's afraid to hear the truth.

I sit for a while with D-man. He opens up a can of Hawaiian Sun Guava Nectar for me and I practically drink it in one swig. I would have preferred some tequila or beer, but under the circumstances, it wouldn't have been right.

"Your dad's been working on his brand oh so long."

"Yah." My father is a lot of things, but he does work hard. The playing-hard part has always gotten him in trouble.

I pull a pencil out of my bun, causing my mess of hair to fall past my shoulders. "Why does the boy have to announce this other label now?"

D-man shrugs. "Maybe because Tommy is on his home turf, the kid thought that he wouldn't take it so bad."

"You know he didn't see Mom yet. And she woke up early to make all his favorite food."

D-man tightens his jaw and wipes the already clean counter. A couple of regulars drive up and take their places at the bar. I'm in no mood to be friendly. I nod my hellos and slip off of my stool.

"Don't go, Leilani," one of them calls out to me.

"Mom's waiting for me," I tell them.

When I'm home, I find Mom sitting alone at the dinner table. Only the fried lumpia is out, and I grab a couple and dip them in the sweet sauce. I sit cross-legged on a chair at the table and munch them down. Onolicious. Grandpop Santiago was a cook in the Navy and taught

Mom how to cook, Filipino and all other kinds of foods. She's a good student.

"Where's the boy?" I wipe my greasy hands on a napkin and wonder if there's any leftover pancit in the fridge.

"Sleeping in your room. He was all worn out and I told him to rest."

"My room?" I think back to this morning and the panties and other clothes I stripped off last night.

"Don't worry, I did clean sweep before I let him in."

Mom is always one step ahead of me. I hear the familiar guttural voices of Japanese actors threatening each other, and then the swish of samurai blades emanating from Baachan's TV down the hall. I figure that both Sophie and Dani are in the room with her.

"Dad not here yet?"

"He texted me that he had something to do on the North Shore."

"Probably at Bamboo Royal." I tell her that's where the other pro surfers are staying.

"Before it gets too late, can you go get him?" My mother doesn't say it, but I know what she's thinking. *What if he starts drinking?*

You serious? I think, but I don't say it aloud. "Should I take the boy?" I ask.

Mom gets up and starts putting plastic wrap over the leftover lumpia. She looks older under the lamplight flooding over our dining room table. All her makeup from this morning has faded away. "Ask him," she says.

I take a peek in my room and Luke is spread-eagle on my quilted bedspread, snoring up a storm. The light is off and some of the words on the Killer Wave shirt are glowing in the dark—*really, Dad?* Sleep is what Luke probably needs right now. He can always take Mama Liu's taxi or whatever to get out to the North Shore. It will cost him an arm and a leg, but that's his problem, not mine.

I grab the keys to the Ford Fiesta hatchback from a hook on the wall below a sign that reads "Please Take Off Your Slippahs." I put on my Crocs and go outside. It's still light out; a strong breeze runs through my hair.

The car is unlocked, and I find Sophie already in the passenger seat. She's like a stealth cat.

"Get out," I tell her.

"Can I go with you?"

I don't have time for this. "Get out," I repeat.

"C'mon."

"Well, you have to promise that you stay quiet. And you have to listen to me or I'm gonna leave you at Hanalei Bay." I tell her to text Mom that she's with me. No sense in Mom worrying about an additional missing Santiago.

I can tell that Sophie's close to tears. "Why you so mean to me? It was better when you were in Seattle."

That hurt, but I let it go. Who says I have no self-control?

By the time we are on the highway, the sun is going down. We travel east and then north, through Līhu'e, where the airport, Costco, and Walmart all are. There's also an old-school stretch where you can find saimin and other local grindz. Next is Kapa'a, which has a historic district filled with touristy shops. Traffic is usually the worst there, and we manage to drive only around ten miles per hour for a long stretch. Sophie starts playing her K-pop songs and I glare at her.

"You nevah say notting about me not playin' my music," she says.

"Use my earbuds." I gesture toward the glove compartment.

At a traffic intersection, I connect my phone to the Focus's audio system. It's SZA all the way. Sophie, my earbuds in her ears, frowns in response to some of the lyrics' obscenities. "Mom says you're not supposed to play that music in front of me."

"Just turn up the volume on your phone," I tell her. I know that I'm being a terrible older sister. I may be contributing to her future hearing loss, but it's a Saturday night and I'm stuck with her for a few hours, so I don't care.

I haven't gone to the North Shore that often. I've been mostly working during the past two months and I don't like making the drive. I've forgotten how gorgeous the sunsets are around here. The burst of orange across the skyline, which bleeds a lavender blue. I think about Travis. He would love it here. We've talked about him coming out in a few months, and it won't be soon enough. We Skype every night at midnight Seattle time, and I figure that I'll be home way before then tonight.

Bamboo Royal is up in the Moloaʻa hills, resplendent with kukui and banyan trees. The largest organic farm on Kauaʻi is here, too, and the rows of vegetables seem to fit naturally in the environment. I can tell that Sophie is also mesmerized by the hills, which are quickly darkening under the sinking sun.

We pass a makeshift sign, "Don't Steal Our Aina," which is painted in red on a white bedsheet, stretched across two wooden posts that look like brooomstick handles. We're used to seeing such messages on Kauaʻi, especially in undeveloped areas like this. Āina means "land" in Hawaiian, but more than just a physical place, it's a spiritual one.

"Hey, did you see dat giant wahine?" Sophie turns around toward the sign we just passed.

Silly sistah, I say to myself. Sophie is the one who also imagined that a real menehune was wandering around our neighborhood. Instead of a mythical little person, it turned out to be a garbage bag blowing through some dead trees.

The bed and breakfast is the only structure on its hill. It looks a little like a Japanese pagoda, and Sophie's mouth falls open when she sees it. I park and get out of the car. A few birds chirp in the dusk. One of our island's wild roosters struts in front of us, probably hoping for some scraps of food. It's not as touristy here as other parts of Kaua'i, so he's the lone one on this property.

"Keep quiet," I remind Sophie, and for once she says nothing back. There are a couple of other cars parked to the side, but no scooter. Not a good sign.

We go up the stairs to an expansive wooden porch that is brightly illuminated by an antique light fixture. On both sides of a pale green door are long patio swings. I rap my knuckles on the door, and when I get no response, I press down on its handle. It's Hawai'i, so it's not locked.

"Hello," I call out. Everything—the floor and the furniture—is made out of a deep cherrywood.

There are voices emanating from a room to the right. Three young people about my age lounge in the airy living room area. Two guys are sitting on a black leather couch with video game controls in their hands. I recognize them—one's a big-deal surfer from O'ahu, Rex Adams. I don't remember the name of the other surfer, but I know that he's from Japan.

"Is Tommy Santiago around?" I ask.

The men barely look up from the game screen.

"Tommy? He lives in Waimea," Rex says. He has long-ish brown hair that is feathered back from his face.

"We know that," Sophie spouts out, and I elbow her in the shoulder.

The woman on a long recliner by the window sits up. "Are you Tommy's daughters?" She has an accent, not quite British, but close to it. "You look a tad like him," the woman says specifically to me. She's got long legs that seem to go on forever. I know women like this. I played volleyball with them.

"Sou, ne." The Japanese surfer nods. He looks high.

"Yes, we are." I introduce myself and Sophie. The woman identifies herself as Celia.

"So Tommy is MIA again," she says. She seems almost happy that my father is missing. "Hey, where's Luke?"

"Had dinner with my family," I explain. Celia must be the girlfriend whom Luke was talking about.

"Why didn't you bring Luke with you?" She's laying claim on her man. *I'm not into him, honey*, I think. *I've got my own in Seattle. Yeah, he's more than 2,500 miles away, but it's not like I'm desperate.*

"He conked out. I figured that he needed the rest."

"He's got to be here by noon," Celia says.

"I'm sure my dad will get him here."

"He better. Your father's not known for being too reliable."

If Sophie weren't around, I would have said something back to her. But I try to hold it together. "Let's go, Sophie," I say.

"Wan wan," the Japanese surfer barks at me.

My eyes lock on his face. "Excuse me?"

He visibly shrinks into the couch. "T-shirt. That's husky dog, *desho*?"

I frown and head for the door. "What a-holes," I mutter.

Rex rises, leaving his game controllers, and follows us out to the porch. He's tall, probably six foot three. "Hey, Nori doesn't mean any harm," he apologizes for his friend. "Is Luke okay? We've all been texting him and he hasn't texted back for a day or so."

"Well, he was traveling," I try to offer as an explanation, although it is plenty weird that he hasn't been communicating with his posse, especially his girlfriend. "I really haven't had a chance to talk to him."

"That's probably for the better." When he realizes how weird that sounds, he adds, "Celia's kind of the jealous type."

Of me? That's plain stupid. Travis, unfortunately, falls in the same category, which makes a long-distance relationship especially hard.

When we are back in the car, I immediately text my dad. I haven't done so in about three months, according to the leftover text messages on my phone. I wait for a few seconds. No response back. This trip has been a complete waste of time.

"I don't like her," Sophie says from the passenger seat.

"Huh?"

"That girl surfer. She dissed Dad."

For once, I can agree with my sister's sentiments. Yeah, Dad's a jerk, but he's our jerk. Santiagos reserve the exclusive right to insult our own.

Sophie nods off during the drive home. I think about putting on my music, but I don't want to disturb her. She's the cutest when she's asleep. She finally stirs when I idle the car in front of our house.

She wipes her eyes with the sleeve of her hoodie. "Aren't you going in? Maybe Dad's back."

"I'm just going to check on the shop. Wanna make sure Sammie closed everything up okay." Since there's been a rash of burglaries on this side of the island, I've been more cautious recently.

Our tiny business district is pretty much dark; the bar is completely closed up. As a one-man operation, D-man doesn't have regular hours, and I remember that he'll be working at the competition early tomorrow morning. But there's light coming out of one establishment, Killer Wave.

I knock on the glass pane on the door.

"Eh, you wen find him?" Kelly lets me inside.

I shake my head. "Nope. He's disappeared. Into thin air. Like always."

"Give him a break. He's trying to turn things around."

Kelly, always the glass-is-half-full kind of guy. I've forgotten how much I've missed his positivity.

He's doing inventory of his rental equipment. On the hardwood floor are pairs of swim fins. He's placed a few damaged goods, a fin with a broken strap and a cracked snorkeling mask, to one side.

"Good you wen come back, Leilani. It's like everyting is how supposed to be."

He gives me one of those looks, and I have to admit that my heart skips a beat. Most of the time we've spent together over the past couple of months has been with Court.

"Well, I'm happy for you two. Court and you," I say awkwardly. "This summer, eh. When you two gettin' hitched?"

He smiles. "Court wants you as her maid of honor. She gettin' round to asking you. Once there's no shibai."

There seems no escaping drama when my dad's around.

Beams of light flash through the window, and then we hear a car engine turning off.

"Who's that?" I ask.

Kelly looks out the window; I follow behind him.

It's a long white van parked in front of the vacant storefront next to Killer Wave.

"Looks like one of those serial killer vans. You know, the ones in those crime shows on Netflix."

"You've been bingeing too much," I say, but I have to agree.

Emerging from the driver's side is a haole guy, with black-framed glasses, slim build, and wearing a loose, lightweight jacket over a white T-shirt. I can't tell for sure, but his hair looks dark and curly.

"He looks like a serial killer," Kelly says.

"You think he's taking over Auntie Lulu's place?"

"Nah, he no look like one baker."

"Just 'cause was one cookie place, no mean going be one now."

"Landlord tells us notting."

That part is definitely true. I am now in charge of paying the bills, and the rent check for the shack goes to some generic limited liability company.

The man pulls out a key, opens the door, and enters the storefront.

"Should we go over there and say howzit?" Kelly asks.

"To a serial killer?"

Kelly flashes his pearly whites and we both laugh.

"Well, this is good fun and all, but I gotta go." With everyone attending the surf competition, I'm pretty much on my own at the shack tomorrow.

"Pekelo gonna mind tings here."

Kelly's competing, I remembered. His older brother, Pekelo, has been filling in for him often, just yesterday, in fact.

Before I leave, I check the front door and the pop-up window of Santiago's. Both are properly locked; everything is safe and sound. On my way back to the car, I can clearly see the license plate on the van. Another Californian trying to find paradise in my hometown.

When I get home, I kick my Crocs off and hang the key on its hook. Only the hall light is on, and I hear light snoring from the girls' room. Everyone is sleeping.

I check my room, and it's empty. Luke must have found a ride to Bamboo Royal on his own. Thank God.

I plop down on the bedspread, which was quilted several years ago by Baachan. It has a purple background with a lavender appliqué in a breadfruit pattern. She made it for me when I left for college in Seattle, and I brought it back with me.

I open up my laptop and see that it's ten o'clock, so 1 a.m. in Seattle. Damn. I didn't realize it was so late. I message Travis on Skype, and we connect. His skin has a greenish tint from the bedroom lamp, but I'm not going to mention it.

"I'm so sorry," I say. "I lost track of time."

I tell him everything that happened today: Dad's arrival with Luke and then his disappearance. The long drive to the North Shore for nothing.

"You can't just do everything your mom wants you to do," Travis says. "You're just enabling her codependence." Travis's mother is a therapist, and I hate when he starts to psychoanalyze me.

"My mom was worried. You mean I'm supposed to

ignore how she's feeling?"

"It's between your dad and your mom. You don't need to get in the middle."

I try to relax my face so it doesn't reveal my anger, but I'm not good at faking anything. "You know that my mom's sick, right? It's not like everything is normal."

"Leilani, Leilani." Travis's voice gets soft. "I'm sorry. I'm not trying to make you feel bad. I was looking forward to talking to you. I was worried about you."

I take a deep breath. "Yeah, sorry about that. It's just that a lot has been going on. What did you do tonight?"

He tells me about an open mic he went to at our favorite coffeehouse. A friend in our apartment building performed stand-up, and I guess he bombed. "He said he really missed that you weren't there. You would have told him how much worse everyone else was and made him feel better." I picture the slick, wet streets and the rows of cool restaurants and bars. I miss Seattle, its dark possibilities, and most of all, Travis.

"Did you manage to have any fun tonight?" he asks.

"Nah. After going to the North Shore, I checked on the shack and then Kelly was at the store—"

"You were with Kelly?"

Oh, no, not this, I'm thinking. Travis knows I dated Kelly once upon a time. "He's just a friend. Like a brother. Manages my dad's rental shop and he's engaged to Court." Travis met Court when she came out to visit me in Seattle.

"So, yeah, he was there, counting snorkeling fins. Really exciting stuff."

Travis grows quiet. He looks away from the screen, half of his face glowing green.

I quickly change the subject. "Waimea is pretty dead

at night. But there's the beach. And it was eighty degrees today."

"I'll take that over bad comedy."

I'm not sure I would, but I grunt in agreement.

"No panic attacks today?"

I shake my head, a bit mad to be reminded of my emotional challenges. The thing is, I really haven't had an attack since I've come home. I'm not sure what that means, but I don't want to think about why. With my father back on Kaua'i, I don't want to think about anything difficult tonight.

When I open my eyes, my room is still dark. It's actually a converted garage, and the window that Grandpop Santiago built for it is only two foot square. I don't mind because it means the sun won't be blinding me at daybreak. I'm not a morning person, and luckily I don't have to go to the shop that early.

It's ten-thirty and I take a quick shower. Afterward, I drag myself into the kitchen in my bare feet and start to make some coffee. Travis has mailed me beans roasted from our favorite Seattle coffee shop. I know Kona beans are world famous, but I need to hang onto something from my old life. Every week Seattle seems to get more distant, as if I had just imagined but not lived those five years away from home.

As I pour hot water into our French press, I notice a note from Mom left on the counter. She's driven Baachan to her ukulele class in Kapa'a and later she, Baachan, and my two sisters will be heading for Cannons Beach on the

North Shore for the competition.

I pour coffee into my UW tumbler, put on my sunglasses, and walk over to the shop. I unlock the door and don't even bother to turn on the lights. Nothing changes in here, and I could probably shave ice with my eyes closed.

My right Croc steps on something squishy and raised high off the floor.

Dammit, Sammie, I think. *Why you have to be so out of it?* I'm messy, too, but I'm not bothered by my own slovenliness.

Then I look down and am frozen in place.

It's Luke, the OC surfer, facedown in a puddle of water.

Chapter Three

BAACHAN SAYS FAMILY IS EVERYTHING, but I know that she really doesn't believe it. It's samurai wish fulfillment promoted in the old Japanese movies she watches. The sword-wielding warriors always talk about *bushido*, or family honor, as they squat and kneel and march around their wooden houses separated by paper walls. But I say it's mostly bullshit.

Our immediate family, especially all the female Santiagos, are super tight, like an unbreakable knot, but go a few branches away on our family tree and all I see are torn-up twigs. For instance, take one of our assistant police chiefs, Sergeant Dennis Toma, whom is supposedly related by marriage to Baachan's older sister over in LA. Those two sisters haven't spoken to each other like maybe ever. And Sergeant Toma, who my father bullied every day in elementary school in Waimea, claims absolutely no connection to us. In fact, I wouldn't be exaggerating to say we are probably on his top-ten list of families he'd like to put behind bars.

I'm getting that vibe now as he sits across from me at our picnic table out front of the shop. He's wearing his dark uniform with four gold stars on each shoulder. His slender fingers are clasped together on the table, right next to a big glob of strawberry sauce. I want to tell him to watch out for the sauce, but I don't think that he'd be open to any kind of helpful warnings from me.

"Tell me one more time," he says.

How many times I gotta tell you, brah, I say silently, but I comply.

I knew that Luke was dead from the get-go. I mean, his face—both his nose and mouth—had been immersed in water. He had a terrible gash on the back of his head, and blood had soaked through his golden hair. I don't know how I did it, but I was able to think enough to get on my cell phone and dial 9-1-1. "There's a dead body on the floor of our business. Santiago Shave Ice. Yah, yah, I know him. Luke Hightower. He's a surfer from California." I gave our address to the dispatcher and was told the police would be on their way.

I ran outside to see if anyone was around. Killer Wave was closed until eleven and, besides, Kelly was on the North Shore. There was a hand-drawn sign on Lee's Leis and Flowers: "Be Back Soon." No one seemed to be next door in Auntie Lulu's place and, besides, I didn't know how helpful this new guy from California could be. I stood outside and waited. I feared that I was going to have a panic attack, but it didn't come. I smoked through my single cigarette and had second thoughts. Maybe Luke was actually alive, holding on to the last bit of life. And here I was, outside smoking a cigarette.

I went back inside, turned on the lights, and gingerly walked toward the body. I could clearly see a pool of liquid around him. I touched the liquid—it was cool to the touch—and smelled my wet fingertips. Odorless and colorless. Was it water? What the hell had happened? I checked our freezer for leaks, but the equipment seemed to be fine. The dispatcher had told me not to touch the body, but still I wanted to make sure that he was dead. Kneeling down, I touched his shoulder. It was stiff and, yes, definitely lifeless.

My story, told the third time, is over. "So then you guys showed up." I fold my arms tightly, as if I'm hugging myself.

One of the officers lifts up the yellow crime tape loosely hung across Santiago's open front door and walks toward us.

"Hey, long time no see," the officer says to me. Andy Mabalot and I had been in the same high school class. He was nice enough—he even invited me to a dance once, but I turned him down. Kelly and I were kind of friend-dating and I didn't want anything to further complicate that relationship.

Sergeant Toma doesn't seem to appreciate small talk, at least that's the impression I get from the way he glares at Andy, who quickly clears his throat. "There was no cell on him," he reports to his superior. Toma writes something in his notebook, sends Andy away to collect some evidence, and resumes his interrogation. "So he was staying at your place."

"He was resting."

"Where, on the couch?" Sergeant Toma asks.

What did that matter? "No, in my bedroom."

Toma furiously writes something in his notebook.

"It's not what it sounds. My mom told him to. I was back here at Santiago's. She was just trying to be nice." The Aloha Spirit is probably a foreign concept in Sergeant Toma's vocabulary. "When I got home from Bamboo Royal, he was gone."

"And you have no idea where he went?"

"I told you. I barely know the guy. I don't even have his cell phone number."

"Your father? He didn't sleep at your house?"

"I dunno," I say. "By the time I got home last night, no

one was up." That wasn't a lie. Toma takes notes on what time I had left Santiago's. "You can ask Kelly Kahuakai," I tell him.

"Don't worry. I will."

Just then a white van rumbles into Waimea Junction's dirt parking lot. "That guy was here last night," I say before even thinking.

"Who?"

The slim haole man in the same hoodie emerges from the driver's side.

"I think he's renting Auntie Lulu's old place."

"I miss her cookies." I didn't realize Andy had returned to the picnic table with Sergeant Toma's bagged evidence.

"I do, too," I exclaim, and Toma lets out another sigh. I try to see what's in the bag, but Toma sends him away. "Officer Mabalot, go over and get an initial statement from him."

Andy nods and heads over to the van. I start to get up, but Toma stops me and says that he has more questions. Just my luck.

"Hightower didn't leave his suitcase at your house?"

I shake my head. "He just came for some grindz and rest, I guess." I remember the luggage we moved into the back of Killer Wave. No need to reveal that to Toma now. Not until I had a chance to get a good look at it.

"Well, we'll have to talk to your mother and the rest of your family. Maybe they'll know when Hightower left your house."

"They are all at the surf competition up at Hanalei. This boy was supposed to be there, too."

Just then my phone vibrates, and I look down to read the text. It's my reminder to order more syrup from our Honolulu supplier.

"Let me see your phone."

"Why?"

"Are you hiding something?"

"No." I reluctantly hand over my phone to Toma.

"What's your password?"

"I'm not going to tell you that."

"I'm going to hang on to this, okay? Until after we talk to your parents."

"That's not right. Don't you need a warrant?" *Law & Order* is one of my favorite TV shows, and I've seen almost every iteration of it, even the episodes made before I was born.

"If you don't want to cooperate. . . ."

I hold my face with my hands. "Take it. I don't care," I lie. "Is that all?"

"For now." He offers me a ride to the North Shore in his squad car, but I decline. All I need is the rest of Kaua'i to see me in the back of a black and white. Leilani Santiago, she hasn't changed much since high school.

I watch as a covered body on a stretcher is carried out to the coroner's jeep. I feel sick to my stomach and can taste the acid of my morning coffee, but not in a good way. Members of the local TV news crew have arrived with their cameras, and I pretend that I'm just a lookie-loo instead of a material witness. After about forty-five minutes, the police officers, including Andy, get into their squad cars. Now I'm at a loss for what I'm supposed to do. One side of the yellow crime tape has come loose and is flapping in the breeze. *No sense in doing business today*, I think. I stay outside, as if Luke's soul is floating somewhere in the shack.

About fifteen minutes later, I see someone on a bicycle wheeling toward me. "Howzit?" It's Kelly's older brother.

Before, everyone called him Pete, but after he came back from military service in the Middle East, he wanted everyone to call him by his Hawaiian name, Pekelo.

He notices the crime tape. "Someting happen?"

I tell my story for the fourth time. "I've never seen a dead body before," I confess.

"You lucky den."

"Not so lucky today."

"You like me call Kūheakapu?"

"Nah, I guess I'm not supposed to talk to anybody until the police get to them first."

"That's messed up. It's not like you wen kill him. You neva, right?"

"Why would I?"

"Seemed like he was the son that your dad nevah had. Least that's what I heard."

"From who?"

"Ah, nobody."

Yeah, right. Probably some of the guys who hang out at D-man's after the sun sets.

"Toma took my phone."

"What? Dat's illegal. He needs one warrant for dat."

"I thought so." I remember the luggage stored in the back of Killer Wave. "Actually, there's something you can help me with." I gesture toward the surf shop and we make our way inside.

The back storage room is just an add-on, done by my grandfather maybe before I was born. The makeshift roof is coming apart, and there's a ring of black mildew in the corner of the ceiling.

"This place is a damn mess. Your dad gotta do someting about it."

"Yeah, if you can keep him still for twenty-four hours."

Underneath a worktable sit two rollaway suitcases. Out of familiarity, I open Dad's maroon one first. I was with him when we went to Costco to buy luggage for college, and he ended up buying a matching one. His is a lot more worn than mine, given all the travel he does.

After I put it on its side and unzip, a bunch of Killer Wave Hawaiian shirts spill out.

"Plenty shirts," Pekelo observes. "Why same kine?"

"It's his brand. Every color in the rainbow. And writing glows in the dark." I hold one up to him. "What you think?"

"Lolo," Pekelo says.

Yup. Just what I had thought. My father has lost his mind. "Pupule, yah. I couldn't stop him. He doesn't listen to me."

"Tommy Santiago, he no listen to anybody. Especially to girls."

That hurt a little, but I also felt vindicated. I wasn't just imagining Dad's slight against my gender.

I hesitate a moment before pulling the zipper on Luke's roller bag, a hard-shell kind decorated with a blown-up Union Jack graphic. Luke was dead and I was invading his privacy. And I'm sure I might be interfering in Sergeant Toma's investigations by taking a peek. But I do it anyway.

Unlike my father, Luke is a light packer. I feel embarrassed to see plaid boxers folded into rectangles à la Marie Kondo.

"The dude's neat," Pekelo says with a hint of respect. His military training has given him an appreciation for uniformity, at least in terms of underwear.

There are T-shirts, shorts, and a couple of short-sleeved shirts, all still donning clothing tags. "All his stuff is new,"

I say.

"This a new Australian brand. Some catalogs for them come in the mail to the shop." Pekelo goes into the retail part of the store and brings back a stack of thick catalogs, both glossy and matte. He dumps them atop the worktable. "Here, dis one."

I quickly leaf through it, and on an inside page is a note from the founder, his photo taken with a familiar woman. "That's Luke's girlfriend. I met her last night. Celia Johnson."

"She's one champion surfer herself," Pekelo comments. "Won the Gold Coast title in Australia."

I feel a pang of sadness. I picture her hearing about the death of her boyfriend. Even though I didn't get a very good first impression of her, I wouldn't wish this kind of bad news on anyone.

A car door slams shut outside. We walk over to the front door to check it out. Our mystery neighbor is leaving in his white van. I wonder what he had to say to Officer Andy.

"Who dat?"

"Not sure. I think he's moving into Auntie Lulu's place. Andy Mabalot questioned him, I think. Kelly and I saw him here last night."

"Damn suspicious," Pekelo says.

I don't have time to chitchat about our mystery neighbor. "I need some wheels to get to the North Shore."

"Kelly took the Toyota or else you could use. How about Mama Liu?"

I hesitate. Money's been tight, plus in my sensitive state, I don't know if I can stomach her erratic driving.

"I'll call Court," Pekelo volunteers, and I'm thankful.

Turns out she was heading back to the shop to pick up some anniversary leis that she needed to deliver. "She goin' to North Shore anyways. She give you one ride."

"Thanks," I say. I don't move from the middle of the Killer Wave sales floor.

"You scared for go back in." Pekelo has me figured out. "C'mon."

I follow him out the door. He rips off the crime tape outside Santiago's and wads it into his fist. Much of the water on the floor has evaporated, but there's still a visible wet spot. Assorted trash, possibly from tourists—a couple of our long blue spoons, a felt purse in the shape of a pizza slice, a red scrunchie, a gold origami crane, and a plastic bowl—are scattered on the ground. If this had been the crew on *Law & Order*, you probably wouldn't have seen all these forgotten bits of evidence. But then, this isn't the island of Manhattan; this is Kaua'i, with a dwindling police force that investigates more stolen bicycles than murders.

"Dis mess, too," Pekelo says.

I try to blame it on Sammie because yah, she should have cleaned the place before closing. Pekelo asks for a bucket, mop, soap, and bleach, and I go through our small kitchen toward the cleaning closet. I pass by our large ice freezer and find that Sammie didn't bother to replace a block of ice that she used. *That girl needs to get her head into work instead of guys*, I think.

Once Pekelo has the cleaning gear, he works quickly. He spreads bleach on one particular spot, and I notice a red liquid leeching out. I feel sick to my stomach again and go outside for a breath of fresh air. I pull down my sunglasses from the top of my head and adjust them over my eyes. What was Luke doing here at the shack? Either he came in the middle of the night or at the crack of dawn. And how did he get in? I had checked the front door and it was locked.

The Lee's red minivan swings in and stops in front of the flower shop. After Court jumps out of the driver's side, I practically run out and leap into my friend's skinny arms, almost knocking her down.

"What happen, Leilani?"

"I'll tell you on da road. Lemme use your phone to get ahold of the fam."

No one seems to be answering his or her phone. Pekelo helps Court load long boxes of leis into the back while I send a group text:

Call me at this number. I'm using Court's phone. Emergency.

Pekelo tells me that he will lock up the shack after he finishes cleaning. As we pull onto the highway, I feel overwhelmed with Pekelo's and Court's kindness. It's then I start to cry, and bits of the story come out in between tears all the way from Waimea to Po'ipū to Līhu'e and, finally, Hanalei Bay.

It's not like me to be all weepy. "I guess you in shock," Court says as I wipe my face on some tissues she has in the car. The tissue box is covered with needlepoint that makes it look like Spam musubi. Court is crafty like that, just like my mom, who does embroidery for friends and family.

"My hanabaddah gettin' all over your phone," I tell her. I try to clean it and my sunglasses with the tissues. Court shakes her head and takes her sticky phone from me without any reservations. "No worry. Your snot is my snot."

"I probably look awful."

"That's da ting, Leilani. With your body, you could walk in a room wid no makeup, maybe covered in hanabaddah, and all da bruddahs be gathering 'round you."

"Dat's so uji." I can't help but crack a smile.

"Sounds gross, but it's true."

"At least I'm not having one of my attacks."

"What's dat?"

"I told you. In Seattle I'd get these panic attacks. No can breathe right."

Court narrows her eyes, as if this is the first she's heard of them.

We've reached Cannons Beach, and Court parks next to some overfilled garbage cans. Feral chickens are furiously pecking at some discarded fast food. "Sorry I can't stay," she says.

"No, no." I blow hard into my wad of tissues and my right ear even pops. "You da best."

"Nah, you da best," Court says.

I jump out of the minivan, noticing a row of police cars. I put on my sunglasses again to mask my swollen eyes. Has Toma broken the news to my family yet? I see some uniformed police officers by the judges' table—a surfboard on top of two sawhorses—in the distance by the shore. On the other side of the beach are the gray roots of a banyan tree. That's the Santiago spot. In fact, Baachan's sitting in an upright beach chair underneath a giant blue umbrella. Laid out below are towels on which open Tupperware containers reveal the last of our Filipino leftovers.

Dad is with Mom on the same towel. She's also safely shaded by an umbrella, sitting in a low lawn chair, her hiking sticks nearby. Wearing a probably recently woven green-palm-leaf hat, Dad is on his side, lazily eating something—maybe lumpia—with his hands. Sophie has her earbuds on and she sits with her knobby knees together while Dani is drawing in the sand with her finger.

I hold this image in my mind. This is a moment in which the Santiagos are happy. A family having a good time at the beach. I know that this is going to end in a matter of minutes, seconds. But it did exist right now.

D-man walks toward me. He looks at me with concern. Somehow he knows what has happened. I grab him by his T-shirt. "Don't tell Toma anyting about what happened with Luke and my dad," I hiss in his ear.

He looks almost angry, or at least defensive. "I'm no snitch, Leilani."

As the uniformed officers descend on the beach, they remind me of black ants seeking their next piece of sustenance. My father, a juicy morsel.

My family finally realizes that the police presence is not routine. My parents look at their phones, exchange glances, and start poking their screens with their fingers.

"I'm here," I say loudly, now only a few feet away. I'm fully aware that I'm the one who will be breaking the rare spirit of 'ohana taking place.

There's no time to beat around the bush. "I found Luke. Dead. On the floor of Santiago's this morning." There's a split second of silence, and all I hear is the familiar roar of the waves.

"No, Leilani, how?" My mother balances herself up in the sand with her hiking stick.

Dad, on the other hand, asks no questions. He puts his face in his hands—they are dark and calloused, the fingernails rimmed with dirt.

In the distance, I see the Japanese surfer Nori, Rex, and Kelly coming out of the water in their wet suits, carrying their surfboards.

A woman with a long stride cuts through the sand toward me. "So there you are," Celia says. "Where's Luke? Your father says he called him to take a taxi. Nobody knows where he is."

"Ah—" Now my tongue seems out of my control. I cannot form words.

"He's dead," Sophie pipes up. I had forgotten that she was there. "He's dead and Leilani found him."

The black ants are now around us, surrounding us. There's the chief ant, Dennis Toma. He calls my father's name and asks him to follow him. He wants to take him and my mother to the station to answer some questions.

"I come, but my wife needs to rest. You can come by the house tomorrow." I give my father props for looking after Mom.

Through this, a guttural scream. It's the girlfriend, Celia. Her beautiful freckled face has become ugly, contorted. Curse words spill out of her, one after another, mostly directed toward my father, who has gotten up and is brushing sand from his shorts. "What the hell did you do to him? I knew you were no good."

Andy goes to her side. She's a head taller than him and, next to her, he almost looks like a child. He says something softly in her ear, and it's like he's put a spell on her. She quiets, and they walk together to one of the squad cars.

"I gotta go with them," my dad announces. He's wearing the same Killer Wave Hawaiian shirt and it looks all wrinkled and worn, as if he has slept in his clothes.

"They're not arresting you, are they?" Sophie asks.

"No, baby." Dad ruffles her hair and places his hat onto her head. "Everything will be okay." He leans down to kiss my mother's forehead.

I feel like throwing up again, but after Dad collects his slippahs and begins to follow Toma, he says to me, "I'm depending on you, Leilani. Keep everyone together."

Dani is now in full-out crying mode in my mother's lap. In the green hat, oversize for her head, Sophie walks out to the parking lot to watch our father being put in the backseat of the patrol car. I lock eyes with Baachan, who remains in her chair. She doesn't look scared or shocked. She is damn pissed, and I can feel the heat of her anger several feet away.

One of my dad's best friends on Kaua'i, Rick Chen, who lives close to Hanalei Bay, comes by and helps us collect our sandy towels. Rick is kind of like Kelly, in that his face rarely shows the worry that he holds inside. "Is it true, Leilani? That the police think your dad killed someone?" They've been so close, like brothers, and we spent a lot of holidays together. Mom says that Uncle Rick knows things about Dad that no one else does.

Behind him is his wife, Auntie Barbara, holding on to a leash attached to their black Labrador, Duke. Even with the sun, Barbara's face looks as pale as an *obake*, a ghost. Her dyed-black hair is swept off her face in a bun held together with a scrunchie decorated in the same pattern of the bandanna that Duke wears around his neck. She's a vet technician, and the Chens probably have at least a dozen assorted animals in their house. I don't know why, but she and Dad have never really gotten along. Maybe she gets in the way of the bromance. Either way, that doesn't affect my relationship with her. She squeezes my shoulder and, letting down Duke's leash, begins to put some of the dirty Tupperware in used ABC Store bags.

"Dad had nothing to do with it," I tell Uncle Rick.

"Tell everyone who thinks different."

"I know that he didn't," Rick says. And he says it with such confidence that for a second I feel a little lighter.

D-man offers to drive a couple of us in his car back to Waimea, but I shake my head. "It'll be tight," I tell him. "But we need to be together."

On our drive home, I put on Israel Kamakawiwoʻole's music. I know it's old-school, but it's my mother's favorite. Somehow his soothing voice and the strumming of the ukulele calm us, even Baachan, and soon she and the girls have dozed off in the backseat.

Mom is still awake in the passenger seat, her hiking sticks in between her legs. "Why do they think he was involved?" she whispers, more to herself than to me. "And where was he? Where could he have been?"

I keep my eyes on the highway. I don't have any answers.

When we get home, I rustle the backseat passengers out. "Everybody gotta bocha tonight," I tell them. Maybe it's because of our Japanese side, but hot baths seem to make everything a little better. The girls are first, and they don't mind sharing the tub. Baachan's next, and she comes out with her hair down and dripping with water, looking like an angry troll who just survived a drowning.

I tell my mother as she gets ready for her turn that I'll wash her back, one of my father's regular rituals. Before my mom goes in, I check the bathroom. As I suspect, it's a mess. The linoleum floor is slick and our flimsy bath mat is soaking wet. *Animals*, I think. I take a boro-boro, holey rug and sop up the water. The last thing I need is Mom taking a tumble. Because our bathroom is usually a disaster, she's careful to keep it free from all her expensive medications, which she stores in their bedroom. After she soaks for about five minutes, I take a soft sponge shaped like a giant bone, push it into the warm bathwater, and scrub my mother's bare back. Mom's skin is like a typical haole's: She has freckles and sun spots all over. It's strange to be doing something she would be doing for me to feel better. For so long, Mom was my Superwoman. The one who was playing beach volleyball with the guys, making and mending clothes, and cooking up the best grindz.

"Oh, that feels so good, Leilani." And then, as if a switch had turned on, Mom breaks down in the bathtub, her tears running into her bathwater. I keep rubbing her back with the sponge. "It's going to be okay, Mom. You know he didn't do it," I say, though not confidently enough to convince myself.

"No, it's the boy," she says. "He was young, with everything in front of him. Who could have done that to him?"

By the time I take my bath, our rickety water heater has stopped producing much hot water at all. My skin feels cold and clammy, and soon I'm starting to get chicken skin. So much for the healing effects of a hot bath. Instead, I feel today's events stick to me even more.

Once changed into an oversize T-shirt, I suddenly realize that I haven't told Travis anything. I open my laptop on top of my bed and try to Skype him, but he doesn't respond. I have to be lame and use Facebook to message him:

Sorry. The police have my phone. A lot of shit has happened. I'm okay. We're all okay. Kinda.

I wait. No immediate response. I lie back on my bed and fall asleep for I don't know how long. I don't have my phone to tell me what time it is. Based on the darkness and silence, it seems late. I take a deep breath and dangle my arm toward the floor by my wall. I feel something. It's hard and smooth. A phone, one that I've never seen before. When I touch the screen, I see the lock-screen image.

It's of Luke Hightower, tanned with a dazzling white smile. He's next to another haole man, older, with thick silver hair. They are inside some building, standing in front of an old wooden surfboard. But wait, is that a scratch on his screen? The nose of the surfboard is dark, but when I take a closer look, there's no mistake. It's a swastika. The two smiling haole men are posed in front of a surfboard decorated with a symbol of Nazi pride.

Chapter Four

I STUMBLE OUT OF MY BEDROOM, trying to process what I've just seen on Luke's phone. Him, smiling next to a surfboard donning a swastika. Was he a white nationalist? I mean, that doesn't make sense. I need some ice cream to get clarity. And a cigarette afterward.

Fortunately, there's still a corner of mango 'n cream in the carton, which I dig out with a teaspoon to make it last. While licking the spoon, I sit on the couch and stare at the full moon visible through our opaque drapes over the window.

Something squeaks behind me.

"Who dat?" I say, accidentally spitting out some precious ice cream.

"Me," Dani steps into the lit hall. She's wearing dad's old University of Hawai'i Wahine T-shirt. It's XL and almost reaches her calves. Her blond, wavy hair is shaped like a tangle of dried seaweed. It's going to be tough to comb it out in the morning.

"I going to the bathroom. Are you okay, Leilani?"

I nod. "How about you?" Besides our dad being taken in for questioning by police, there was the shock of Luke's death. The golden surfer had been at our family table, eating a mouthful of pancit the night before.

Dani nods.

"Come ova here," I tell her.

Dani slowly approaches, as if she's slightly scared of what I'm going to say. "You and Sophie cleaned off the surfboards that Dad and Luke brought ova yesterday."

She nods again, and I notice some sleep stuck in the corner of her eyes.

"What did they look like?"

"They were boards I had never seen before. One was made out of wood."

I pick up Luke's phone, tap the screen, and hold it in front of her. "Was it dis one?"

Dani squints and nods. "Yeah, it had that funny mark on it. Sophie said that it was a bad mark, but I didn't know why. What does it mean?"

I frown, trying to understand why my dad and Luke would bring over such a board to the Islands. "I explain later," I tell her.

"I really gotta go shi-shi." Dani's hands are clasped in front of her giant T-shirt.

"Yah, sorry," I say and let her go.

I finish off the ice cream and wash out the empty carton so that the bugs don't come. After smashing it into the trash, I look into my parents' room. Mom is sleeping alone in the bed. Dad hasn't come home yet. Toma, that friggin liar. He said that he was taking my Dad in for questioning, not that he was going to spend a night in the police station.

Based on Luke's phone display, it's midnight and I probably should handle this in the morning, but I can't sleep, anyway. I take a couple of keys off of their hooks underneath the "Please Take Off Your Slippahs" sign and put on my Crocs. Once I'm in the Ford, I take out a lighter and a fresh pack of cigarettes from the glove compartment. Once the car is running, I open the window and blow out some smoke into the moist night air.

Once I reach Waimea Junction, I see that the mystery man's white van is outside Aunt Lulu's old place, which is lit up. *Is this guy some kine vampire?* I say to myself. *What's he doing on Kaua'i, anyhows?*

I park my car in front of Lee's Leis and Flowers, pull out a flashlight from the car door pocket, and quietly creep up the wooden stairs of Killer Wave.

I go in without turning on the light and use the flashlight to get to the back. There are the same five, six surfboards lined up in a row. Mostly rentals. I don't see anything wooden. On the floor, underneath the worktable, I spot the two black surfboard cases, next to the rollaways. Both empty. I aim the flashlight in different corners of the back room to make sure that I haven't missed anything.

Through the back window, the grim face of the haole neighbor stares back at me from outside. I let out an f-bomb and then regain my composure. I go to open the back door, but he beats me to it.

I tighten my grip around the flashlight as he enters the back room.

"I'm not going to hurt you," he says. I guess he noticed my fighting stance.

"Damn, you scare me," I tell him.

"Well, you scared me." He adjusts his glasses. "You're the girl with the shave ice shop. One of the Santiagos."

I snap on the light. "I'm Leilani."

"Sean Cohen," he introduces himself. He has huge brown eyes behind his black-framed glasses. His hair is a mass of dark curls. "I've moved in next door. I'm from California." Tell me something I don't know. "Sunnyvale. It's near San Jose."

Never heard of it, but I nod my head as if I have.

Since we are getting friendly, I feel bold enough to ask him outright, "Whatchu doin' here in Waimea, anyway?"

"I'm here to make soap."

Oh, one of those *Mainland people*, I think. Made some coin there and then come to Hawai'i to produce something that nobody really needs. "I saw you movin' in," I tell him. "This is my father's place, too."

"Then why are you sneaking around with a flashlight?"

"Well, I didn't want to bother you."

"That didn't work." He says it with a squirt of sarcasm. I like sarcasm and am warming up to my neighbor, who I have to admit is pretty hot up close. "I may be on edge because of what happened."

I look down. "Yeah, I'm the one who found him."

"I heard."

"The police told you?"

"Well, it's been all over the local news, too. They even said that they may have a person of interest in custody."

Not my father, I hope. "The police don't know the whole story." Seeing Sean's confused expression, I say, "He brought over a bizarre surfboard. I'm wondering if that's connected with his murder."

"That must be some surfboard."

I remove Luke's phone from my pocket and turn it on. It still has about thirty percent juice. "Look what's on the nose of the surfboard."

Sean pulls off his glasses, studies the image, and frowns. "That's not what I think it is. . . ."

I nod my head.

The glasses are back on his face. "Why would Luke and his father be seen with a swastika?"

"So it is his father? You know them or someting?"

"Know of them. The father owns some property on Kaua'i. I doubt that he's a white nationalist, but I guess you never know."

Could Luke be a Nazi lover? I ponder that for a moment. Why would he be hanging out with my dad, a Filipino Japanese? Maybe he was being unduly influenced by some Grand Wizard type, like his father. Maybe his father convinced Luke that he couldn't accept a sponsorship from Killer Wave.

"I don't think Luke was that type of guy. But I really don't know much about him." I think back to his crowd in Bamboo Royal. None of them seemed the hater type. Except for maybe the girlfriend. You didn't want to cross her. All I knew was this was all way beyond me. "I probably need to get his phone to the police. And tell them about the missing surfboard."

"Hey, before you give it to them, can I get a picture of the surfboard?"

"Why?" *What was this guy after?*

"I'm always on the lookout for haters."

That's kind of a weird thing to say, but I don't challenge it. "Sure, go ahead." I touch the screen and hold out the phone.

After he takes his photo, he says, "I can drive you over. Where's the police station? In Līhu'e?"

"Nah, too humbug." I don't want to be a burden. Plus, I'm a little scared about going into that white van.

"Let me help you. We're neighbors now."

Against my better judgment, I agree. I know that Travis wouldn't approve. Neither would Kelly or Pekelo. But they aren't here, and despite their concerns, I can take care of myself.

I remember Luke's suitcase and bring that with us, too. The whole drive over, I also cling the flashlight tightly. If Sean tries anything, he'll find a flashlight in the middle of his Adam's apple.

Sean's GPS takes us to the Lihue Police Station, not far from the airport and Walmart. In the darkness, it reminds me of a haunted museum. Outside, it looks grand, but inside it is anything but, I can tell you that firsthand.

Sean pulls Luke's rollaway as we enter the station. Since it's the middle of the night, it's quiet, and it seems like the receptionist prefers it that way. I want to ask about my father's whereabouts but figure that I can work up to it. I take a chance and ask for Andy.

"It's important. I have evidence related to the murder of Luke Hightower," I say in my most authoritative voice.

The receptionist looks me up and down and checks out Sean. "One minute," she says, and then she gets on the phone.

Could Andy be here so late? I wonder. Based on all their recruitment advertisements, I know that the police force has had a lot of open vacancies.

Andy appears from a doorway in back of the reception area. "Whatchu doin' here in da middle of the night?"

I place the phone on the counter.

"What dis?"

"Luke's phone. I found it tonight. It was underneath my bed. He must have dropped it before he left the house." I press the button to turn on the screen and point to the lock-screen image.

Andy doesn't seem to register the swastika on the surfboard. Instead, he's more fixated on the older man. "Dat's his faddah," he says, confirming what Sean told me. "Sergeant Toma at the airport with him to pick da wife up."

Before Andy can claim the phone, I put my hand over it. "I'll give you dis, but I want *my* phone back. You guys don't have a warrant for it, and Toma shouldn't have taken it."

"I betta check with him first."

"Andy, do you want this piece of evidence or what? I brought his suitcase here and everything."

Andy bites his lip. "Okay, lemme check with the other assistant chief."

"And there's another thing. Where's my father? Is he under arrest?"

"We told him he was free to go home, but he said that he was fine sleeping in the jail cell for a night."

That was plain pupule. I would think Andy was lying, but knowing him since high school, he wasn't that kind of guy.

"Why you wen hold him for so long? And why you make him look guilty in front of everyone at the beach?"

Andy's face becomes flushed. He knows that the police had mishandled the situation at Cannons Beach but still tries to defend their actions. "Some newlyweds saw the news about Luke Hightower and came to the station to report dat you faddah had a fight with him."

"It wasn't a fight. Just disagreement."

"Whatever it was, dat's motive right there."

I start to remember sequences of my favorite *Law & Order* episodes. "Where da murder weapon, den?"

"Yah, we still looking into it."

"Tell my dad we're here to take him home."

"You hangin' out with him now?" Andy asks, gesturing at Sean, who was sitting on a bench with Luke's rollaway beside him.

"He gave me a ride, okay? Just being neighborly."

I think Andy rolled his eyes a bit. What does he care who I spend my time with?

"Waitaminute," he tells me before he goes off to talk to his higher-ups. Toma's not going to be happy that he's not being consulted, but that's his problem, not mine.

I sit next to Sean on the bench. "I think they're going to let my dad go."

"That's great," he says. "That's what you wanted, right?"

Just then the doors of the station open, and it's Toma, followed by an older haole couple. They look beleaguered; the woman's shoulders are bent over as the man holds on to her bent arm, as if he is holding her up. He has a head full of silver hair. I realize it's the man in the photo with the swastika surfboard, the father.

When the woman sees the rollaway next to us, she snaps to life. "That's my son's suitcase."

Toma narrows his eyes. He obviously is not thrilled to see me. "What are you doing here, Leilani?"

"We brought this." I gestured toward the Union Jack rollaway. "And I found his phone underneath my bed." Luke's mother and the man give me a side eye and I hear how awful that sounds. "No, it's not—"

"Mr. and Mrs. Hightower, please go down the hall to the open conference room. I'll be with you in a few minutes." The father, like a predator bird, locks eyes on me, and I feel chills going down my spine. Chicken skin all over. Toma waits until the couple is a hundred yards away before dealing with me.

"So that's the father," I observe and exchange glances with Sean, who also seems to have recognized him from the photo on Sean's phone.

Toma crosses his arms. There are bags under his eyes that I haven't noticed before. "This is none of your business, okay? Turn in Luke's things and go."

"I'd take a good look at his phone," I tell him. "And the surfboard that he brought over, it's gone now." I lower my voice. "It has a swastika on it. Maybe someone stole it."

"We don't need a Nancy Drew on this. I've been doing this work for twenty years now." And he probably has ambitions to be the next chief.

"I'm waiting for my dad. You haven't charged him with anything, right? He should be able to go. And I'm getting my cell phone back." I want to say, *I know my rights, Sergeant Toma*, but I'm actually just learning about them now.

"I know your father had something to do with this." He points his index finger at me. It's a bit crooked, like he had broken or dislocated it in the past. "He hasn't been telling anyone the whole truth. But I'll find out what he's hiding." After that threat, he leaves, the leather belt holding his assorted weapons squeaking as he makes his way down the hall.

I sit back down on the bench.

"He doesn't like you much," Sean says.

"We have history. And believe it or not, we're related. Not by blood, though."

Sean looks at his phone and scrolls through his messages. What kind of texts would a soap maker receive in the middle of the night?

Finally, Andy appears in the reception area, and my father a few steps behind him. Dad's hair, like Dani's, is a tangle, and his goatee has grown into a beard. As he gets close, he smells ripe; it's obvious he hasn't bocha for some time now.

62 ICED IN PARADISE

"Who's he?" Dad asks about Sean as he rolls the suit-case toward Andy.

"He's in Aunt Lulu's spot. He makes soap."

"Eh?" Dad doesn't look too impressed.

"Forget about that. He drove me down here. Luke's parents are here."

Dad's face becomes gray, the color of ash. "I told the mother I take care of the son." His eyes are bloodshot, like the times he had been drinking.

"And here's your phone." Andy returns my cell, and it feels good to have it back in the palm of my hand. *Come to Mama*, I think. It's silly to have emotion about an inanimate object, but that phone is my connection to Travis and the rest of the world. I try to check my texts, but the phone is completely dead.

As I promised, for this phone exchange, I surrender Luke's phone to Andy, its battery level now at eighteen percent. Once we are in the van, my father sits in the front passenger seat. He doesn't bother to say anything to Sean. No thank-yous, no howzits. We ride in silence, and I watch the moon bounce light over the ocean in the distance.

I direct Sean to my house, but he seems to know exactly where I live. Waimea isn't big, but he's a newcomer, and I wonder if he knows more about us than he is telling me.

As soon as he stops by our run-down mailbox, Dad opens the passenger door and jumps out.

"Tanks," I quickly say to Sean as I get out and start running after Dad. I'm quick enough to grab the tail of his Killer Wave shirt. In the full moon, some of the writing is glowing.

"What?" My father is irritated to be caught by me.

"Before we go in, I need to know some things."

He waits, scowling in his typical way.

I readjust my weight from one leg to the other. "Where were you? The night Luke was killed."

"What, you da police now?"

"Dad, I deserve an answer. I went all the way to the North Shore to track you down last night."

"I went surfing. Used a stick outside one of the shacks in Hanalei Bay." *Borrowed* would be a generous word. Some would say *steal*.

"All night?"

"When I got tired, I slept underneath the banyan tree." That would explain the sand caked in his hair. But do I believe him?

"I nevah kill him, Leilani. I was mad, but I wouldn't have killed him."

"By the way, his surfboard is missing."

"What surfboard?"

"One of the surfboards he brought over. The wooden one. It had a swastika on it."

"Who knows about it?"

"Andy and Toma, too, if he bothered to listen. Maybe the one who took the surfboard was the one who killed him."

"Leilani, stay out of dis," Dad says. "You not helpin'." He opens the screen door and goes inside, leaving me alone outside. Somewhere in the neighborhood, a wild rooster crows in the still darkness, as if searching for someone to hear him.

Chapter Five

I DON'T SLEEP WELL THAT NIGHT. I do have some dreams, and I remember one with Luke. He's alive, only his hair is brown instead of blond. He's wearing shorts and a Killer Wave shirt. He's at Pakala Beach, a little southeast of Waimea. He's walking toward the Infinities surf break in his clothes and without his board. "Luke, come back," I call out. But he doesn't hear me over the roar of the surf. He keeps walking, his brown hair barely visible as the waves pound over him until he is completely submerged.

I wake up groggy, and I don't want to move. I can hear the padding of footsteps, the frenetic, hyper steps of probably Sophie and the sure-and-steady ones of Dani. They are getting ready for school. Mom tells them to hurry up, and the toilet is flushed. More light steps on the linoleum and then the bang of the screen door. There are some sounds coming from the kitchen, the clang of dishes and maybe silverware. I smell coffee and pull myself up, grabbing the quilt that Baachan made for me and wrapping it around my shoulders. I fell asleep while my phone was recharging, and now I see a solid wall of text messages. I'm going to need some coffee to get through them.

Baachan is sitting at the kitchen table with the cup of hot green tea that she always drinks in the morning. The paper square of the tea bag hangs from her handleless Japanese mug, and steam covers the surface of her reading glasses. Dad is in one of the other chairs with a mug of coffee, most likely black, the way I drink it, too.

"Howzit," I murmur and leave my phone on the kitchen table as I go over to the coffeemaker. I take my tumbler out of the plastic dish rack and fill it up about halfway.

"Mornin', Lei-ani." Baachan doesn't have her dentures on, so her words sound muffled.

Dad doesn't bother to say hello and instead presses the remote for our tiny TV on the kitchen table. Thankfully, instead of any news updates on Luke's murder, there are mostly traffic reports and talk about some kind of festival this weekend. The news people like to keep it light on Monday morning.

I scroll through my texts. There are quite a few from Dad, actually, asking me if I know where Luke is. Travis has texted me a few times, asking me if I have my phone now. I text him back:

I have my fone. Ill call u later.

He immediately answers me back. *K*

His terseness probably means he's in a meeting.

"You wan toast?" Baachan's on her feet, and I see that she's wearing her usual flowered muumuu.

"Nah, I'm good. I betta go to the shave shack. Not good to be closed so long."

"Wait. We goin' wid you. We decided," Baachan says.

I tell them that I've left the Ford at the shack, but the walk doesn't dissuade my grandmother from insisting that she come with me.

I change into a fresh T-shirt and go to the front door to get my Crocs. Baachan is in the same muumuu but now wearing her teeth, which she bares like a pit bull. She's carrying a straw bag. I try to reach for it, but she wrestles it

away and puts it under her arm. Dad, thankfully, has show-
ered and shaved the sides of his beard. Instead of a Killer
Wave aloha shirt, he's wearing one of the Santiago Shave
Ice T-shirts that Dani had designed earlier this year.

We walk on the grass by the side of the road, my father leading the way. We pass red volcanic rocks arranged
as property borders and enjoy the shade of the almond trees
with their paddle-like leaves and white flowers. There are
koa trees with their spindly branches stretching out to the
sky and, in the distance, green hills that lead up to Waimea
Canyon.

Across the highway is our Ford, parked outside Lee's
Leis and Flowers. And next to it is Santiago's. Before I
go in the shack, Baachan stops me. "We pay respects," she
speaks into the screen door, as if she's making an announcement to some spirit being.

Dad is already inside, checking the floors and the corners of the shack. "Pretty clean." He sounds surprised.

"Pekelo helped us out and made sure everyting was
back to normal," I tell him.

From her straw bag Baachan brings out some incense—I didn't even know she had some—and an empty
tea mug, this one chipped. She places the mug on the floor
next to our counter and fills it with assorted seashells that
we leave around the house. She sticks the incense in the
mug, the shells holding them in place. "Lighter." She extends her arm to me and I dig out a plastic one from one of
our junk drawers.

"Is this some kine of Buddhist thing?" I whisper to
Dad.

He shrugs his shoulders but keeps his distance, as if to
honor Luke's memory.

I remember the lei that Court had brought over and retrieve it from the fridge. I wind it around the cup, and Baachan approves. She puts her hands together and bows toward the altar. We are all remembering Luke in our own way.

Dad meanwhile continues to check the condition of his business. He goes into the kitchen area where our ice freezer is stored. He examines the rows of ice blocks in round molds through the glass cover. "We missin' one."

"Sammie must have used it up and forgot to replace. I'll talk to her about it."

Dad looks right and left and underneath the table. There's a crate where Pekelo had placed the odds and ends he had found on the floor. The pizza purse is empty of any coins. The origami crane looks like something Court could have folded for an anniversary. A red scrunchie features an embroidered dog, my mother's handiwork. Pekelo's even made a sign, "Lost and Found." "Don't see shave ice mold anywhere," Dad says.

Dammit, I say to myself and recheck my phone. I hadn't heard anything from Sammie in a couple of days. No texts or voicemails from her, despite everything that happened yesterday.

I text her:

Howzit? Haven't heard from u. U comin to work today, right? We open.

I wait. Usually Sammie texts me back immediately, even when she's in a class. An exam would be the only exception.

I go one step further and call her. My call goes straight to voicemail. I leave a message, asking her to call me as soon as possible.

"Someting wrong?" Baachan notices my aggravation.

"I haven't heard from Sammie since Sunday. And she's not texting me back."

"Call her mom, then."

I try not to bother the mother. I know her and Sammie's relationship can run hot and cold. But we need her to come in for the swing shift tonight. Plus, I can't stand when people ghost me.

Her family still has a home landline, so I call it.

A woman answers it. "Hallo."

"Hello, Mrs. Nunes? Yah, this is Leilani Santiago."

"Oh, I heard what happen. You folks okay?"

"Yah, it was real terrible. But we back in business."

"Sammie was so upset. Nice you give her time off."

"Huh?"

"Turns out she picked up extra hours at college Student Life Center. All worked out."

"Oh, yah, worked out."

"You want me to tell her someting?"

"Uh, no. I'll find her myself."

So, Miss Sammie, whatchu tellin' your maddah? I say to myself. I inform my father and Baachan that I need to go and talk to Sammie. and they assure me they can handle things at the shack.

Luckily Kaua'i Community College, or KCC, isn't that far. The building part of the school is small, but the land itself is spacious. I drive past green taro fields and rows of other crops that the agricultural students have planted. Sammie somehow got into the two-year nursing program, which is supposed to be competitive, but based on the little studying she does, she's either a genius or barely treading water.

The school is minuscule compared with UW, yet seeing young people wearing book bags, either walking or riding skateboards or scooters, makes me feel a bit nostalgic for that time. Life was so easy when I was at UW. But it was also so brutally lonely. I felt so out of place, so stupid. My classmates had read the classics in high school, passed their AP tests in Calculus. I, on the other hand, was seeing a tutor once a week to learn how to write a college essay. My tutor was even giving up on me. "What do you want to do in the future, Leilani? Do you want to spend the rest of your life on your little island?"

There was no right answer to his question. Kaua'i is 'ohana, home, family, the healing power of the sea. But it's also a very little island, population close to 70,000 people, if you didn't count the tourists. (And we never count the tourists.) Undergrads alone at my university were about half that number.

KCC, in comparison, has barely 1,000 students, the size of most Mainland city high schools. Both Kelly and Court went there and, in the past, I've gone to a few special events on campus. I know the Student Life Center, where Sammie is supposedly working. It's housed in a two-story orange-tannish building. I park the car and head up to the second floor.

There are a couple of Ping-Pong tables, a counter for coffee and drinks, and a bunch of couches where a few students lounge with their laptops. Sitting on one of the couches is Sammie. She's talking to one of her male class-mates, so she doesn't notice me at first. But her companion looks up at me and she finally does, too.

"Whatchu doing here?" She doesn't seem that thrilled that I am there.

"So dis work?"

The guy who was sitting next to Sammie decides that this is a good time for him to leave. *Smart bruddah.*

"I check out Ping-Pong paddles and stuff."

"Why haven't you been returning my texts and calls?" Sammie's cell phone, in fact, is right at her side, like an additional appendage.

"Ah—"

"And I heard from your maddah that I gave you time off."

"You talked to my mom?" Sammie is starting to look desperate.

"Why you avoiding me?"

Sammie looks toward one of the windows, and I think I see a red-footed booby bird flying by.

"Sammie."

She makes eye contact with me, and I see that she's crying.

"What's goin' on?"

"That guy, the surfer, Luke. We made plans to meet up Saturday night. At the shack."

I'm both impressed and shocked that Sammie could make such an impression on a guy in such a short time. I mean, it only took minutes for her to serve him that rainbow shave ice.

"He told me that he had never spent much time in Waimea. Always Poʻipū and North Shore. He gave me his number. Told me I should call him." Noting that look on my face, Sammie protests, "It's not what you tink, okay? I was just tryin' for be nice."

I sit down on the couch next to Sammie, the same spot where her friend had been. I want her to keep talking to me.

And she does. "Things were kind of slow around eight o'clock, so I gave him a call. He was super upset. His girl-friend had been cheating on him and she was textin' him. He didn't know what to do."

"What?"

"Yeah. He said it was super complicated and he couldn't go over it on the phone. So I told him that I would meet him at the shave shack after I closed up. I would have to go home first to show my face, but I would leave the back door open for him. He just shouldn't turn on any lights, because I know how you get about that."

"And did you meet him?"

"I couldn't. My mom was watching me like a hawk. So I texted him to tell him that I couldn't make it."

"Sammie, the police have his phone. They are gonna be able to get his text and calls, and they will see that you were supposed to meet with him."

"But I nevah."

"You can tell them that. But you need to go to them first. Tell them everything that happened."

"My mom's gonna be so upset."

"Sammie, dis murder, okay? Dis not just sneakin' out of the house. Serious, you understand?"

Sammie nodded her head.

"You know where the police station is, right? Not far from the airport. See Andy Mabalot. I think he has a younger sister your age."

"Oh, Teresa Mabalot? I know her." The personal connection seems to immediately reassure Sammie, who is a social butterfly.

"And come in at three to work your shift. We need you. More than eva."

Sammie nods. "I'll be there."

"Oh, by the way, don't forget to fill up the ice, okay?"

"I always do, Leilani."

"One of the molds is missing from the freezer."

"I didn't use it. Just the leftover ice was enough."

Strange, I think. Then what happened to that ice?

As I walk back to the car, my phone dings. A text from Emily:

How's it been with Dad?

Shit, I think. She has no idea about all that's happened. I sit on the grass near my parked car and call her back. She answers and I go into the long, sordid story.

"Should I try to come home?"

"No, Emily, you stay. Notting you can do here." I'm blunt, but it's true. One less Santiago on Kaua'i means one less person to worry about.

There's a couple in hiking gear eating shave ice at the picnic table when I arrive back at Santiago's. I expect my father to be behind the counter, but it's Mom with Baachan at her place behind the cash register.

"Where's Dad?" I ask.

"He can't handle it. People lookin' at him like he's a killer."

It's probably all in his mind, I think, but don't say anything aloud. I notice twin musubi wrapped in nori on the counter. "For me?" How did my mother know that my stomach was rumbling?

"Tuna mayo."

"You read my mind!" I take hold of one and take a huge bite through the crunchy dried seaweed, soft rice, and then the creamy and salty canned tuna mixture. *I'm in heaven!*

Through bites of my lunch, I tell both of them to go

home. "Get some rest. I can handle."

They both hem and haw, but I tell them Sammie is coming in around three. I don't get into her whole situation with Luke right now. She needs to take care of that on her own with the police. Baachan looks like she's ready for a nap, so finally she leaves her perch to be driven back home. This situation with Luke has taken a toll on all of us.

After I finish my second musubi, I walk over to the spot where Luke's body had lain. Someone's moved this morning's altar to a table by the door, and thankfully the tuberose smell overtakes the leftover scent of the incense. Incense always reminds me of funerals and death. The floor is now clear, the wood even lighter where the blood stains were, thanks to Pekelo's generous application of bleach. I remember the cool water underneath Luke's body. That's when I finally realize: The murder weapon must have been the missing ice block.

Could ice kill? A solid shave ice block weighs two, three pounds, about the same as one of my mom's weights. With the right amount of force and angle, it could be used to knock someone out. At least I think I saw something like that on an old *Law & Order* episode.

The door opens and I go around the counter, getting ready to serve. It's the next-door neighbor, Sean, wearing the same hoodie.

"Eh, hello," I say.

He nods his greeting.

"I want to apologize for last night—well, I guess this morning. My Pops wasn't too nice. And me, neither."

Sean barely acknowledges what I've said. "I did some online research on the swastika surfboard," he announces.

"Oh, yah?" The soap maker certainly has a gung-ho side

to him. I had almost forgotten about the swastika.

"Did you know that the swastika symbol can mean something good? Before the Nazis took it over. Like to Buddhists and Hindus."

I pause. I recall being in my Baachan's temple during the Obon festival in elementary school and seeing something that looked like a swastika but reversed. My grandmother couldn't explain why but told me to ask my teacher, Mrs. Shirota, but I forgot. "I think there was something like a swastika in my grandmother's temple."

"It's a super-ancient symbol and stood for good luck—that is, before the Nazis co-opted it."

"So Luke's surfboard was made before World War II?"

Sean nods.

"There was a California building company that started making surfboards in 1932. The swastika was their logo. They changed it up later."

Somehow I feel relieved. I didn't like thinking ill of the dead.

"That surfboard is very valuable," he says.

"What do you mean, valuable?"

"Collectors may pay five figures for one that is in good condition."

Five figures—like $10,000? Pupule.

"So maybe my theory is right—that someone stole the surfboard, and Luke fought them off and got killed in the process," I say.

"Except why was his body in your place?"

"Maybe they saw him and killed him and took his surfboard?"

"That's a real possibility."

"Eh, high five." I put my palm up. At first Sean looks

confused, and then he slaps my palm with his. His palm feels baby soft. I can't believe he's made much soap with all those chemicals.

"Tanks for looking up all that information. I could have, too, but there's a lot of drama in my life right now."

"It's personal," Sean says, and I don't quite register what he means. "I have my eye out for Nazis."

Okay, whatever, I think. All I care about is figuring out what happened to Luke so the police case can be closed for good.

When Sammie arrives—only five minutes late, which means early for her—I go home.

Mom is outside on the porch sitting on a papasan chair. In her lap is a bowl of green mangoes, which she is starting to peel. We used to have three mango trees on our property, but now we have only one. The fruit that it produces is not particularly impressive, but good enough for some things.

"Pickled mango?" I ask, taking a seat on a beer crate next to her.

Mom nods. "I was actually wanting to talk to you," she reveals. "To talk to you about your father."

She stops peeling and looks directly at me. "He didn't do it, Leilani. He was at a meeting on the North Shore."

"What kind of meeting?"

"AA."

Alcoholics Anonymous. "I didn't know that he was going to that."

"Yeah, after your graduation. I told him I would take the girls and leave him. Go back to California to my parents' house."

"You wouldn't have done that." I know that my mother doesn't get along with her parents, and it's partially because

of me. Because I was conceived and born, the first of the
Santiago brood. Because of me, Mom dropped out of col-
lege and abandoned her dreams to play volleyball in the
Olympics.

"No, I would have. For your sisters' sakes. I was only
sorry that I didn't threaten him sooner. That you had to go
through so much."

My eyes sting and I blink away my tears. At least someone noticed.

"The pressure of everything. His Killer Wave brand.
The competition. Being back home with me. It was getting
to him, so he figured that he had to go to a meeting."

"You figure that there would be a closer meeting."

"Rick's his sponsor here."

"Rick's in AA, too?" Damn, is every man around us an
alcoholic?

"So your father has an alibi," she says, as if she is testi-
fying in a trial. He was at an AA meeting."

"But until when?"

"Leilani!" My mom is upset that I'm not accepting this
piece of news as proof of my father's innocence.

"I'm just sayin'." I don't want to excite my mother any
more, and I get up to go inside. In the living room, Dad is
playing video games with Sophie. They are both so absorbed
in their game that they don't even notice that I'm there. I
pour myself some iced tea from the fridge and retreat to my
bedroom. I need to let Travis know what is going on.

Once I get him on the phone, I apologize. I hate when
people ghost me, and this is what I do to him. When I tell
him that I literally stumbled over Luke's body, Travis freaks
out. He now gets how the past couple of days have been so
disruptive, why I haven't been able to talk to him.

"I wish I was there for you," he says.

"I know you would be if you could—"

Our tiny house now seems to be shaking, and I hear the low voices of adult men. "Wait, let me call you back," I tell Travis, ending the call before he can even say okay.

When I get to the living room, I see five police officers—Sergeant Toma, Andy, and three others whom I recognize but don't know by name.

"What's going on?" I ask, but no one is bothering to reply. Mom's arms are crisscrossed over her chest, her hands clutching her drooping shoulders.

"We were able to look into your bank records," Toma says. "Your Killer Wave account isn't doing that well. And a witness claimed that you were always hitting Luke up for money?"

"Dat's not true," my dad responded.

"And we know all about the surfboard. How you sold it to a dealer in Kapaʻa. For $15,000."

I can't remain quiet. "No, that was Luke's surfboard," I say.

"Yeah, but your father told the dealer to make the check out to him. Really interesting."

I wait to hear Dad's protest. That maybe he was acting as Luke's sales agent or something. And, besides, he's supposed to have an alibi, right?

Instead, Dad rises from the couch. "Look, I come wid you. Just don't take me out in handcuffs."

"No, Daddy, no." Sophie hangs on to my father's leg, as if she's a three-year-old. I hate to see her like this.

Toma relishes what he has come here to say: "Tommy Santiago, you are charged with the murder of Luke Hightower."

Andy follows up by reciting my father's rights. His voice is low, barely audible, and Toma admonishes him to speak up.

This is not real, I think. *This can't be happening.* I can't move or speak as the five officers lead my father out of our house, stepping over some overturned green mangoes on our porch and down the stairs.

Sophie, on the other hand, is as fast as lightning. "My father's not guilty," she calls out from our porch over the flattened tall grasses in our front yard.

I wish that I could be that sure.

Chapter Six

"I BET THAT THEY WEN TRUMP UP some charges, just cuz they gotta answer to dat haole guy, what, Mr. Hightower," Kelly says. The tone of his voice was so un-Kelly-like that I had to do a double take to see if somehow Pekelo had entered his younger brother's body.

Court, who helps Kelly with accounting, remains silent as she goes through some of the Excel files for this month's rentals.

I place one side of my face on the display table, next to a stack of catalogs. It's like I can't hold my head up anymore. We had returned from Dad's arraignment this morning. The three of us, my mom, D-man, and Baachan. We told Baachan that she didn't have to come, that it was perfunctory, but she insisted. "Dat's my boy, my only child."

Even Rick had showed up from the North Shore. Rick was the one who got Dad an attorney, a chubby haole man from Līhu'e who didn't seem stupid yet didn't look sharp enough. He certainly wasn't like those legal eagles on *Law & Order* in their crisp navyblue suits and wingtips. Instead, he wore a wrinkled, wilted brown suit and rubber-soled loafers. And his last name was Brown, no lie.

In the front row sat Mr. and Mrs. Hightower. The mother, whose hair and skin seemed like the same color, clutched at a tissue, which became a tight ball by the end of the proceedings. Mr. Hightower, on the other hand, raised his head high, an alert eagle waiting for a mouse to scurry across his path. He gazed my way a couple of times. The district attorney was a woman who had ordered flowers from Lee's Leis, but this morning she acted like she lived in a different world from us.

Dad's lawyer and the district attorney went back and forth on bail. The DA claimed that my father shouldn't be given bail because he was a flight risk, as he traveled to so many countries for work. Mr. Brown countered that Dad was a family man with four young daughters and a sick wife (yeah, he worked that in) and wouldn't abandon them. At first, bail was set at $1 million—I almost fainted when I heard that—and somehow Mr. Brown got it down to half a million. I didn't know how bail works, but after the hearing, D-man told Mom that he would take care of it, somehow.

My phone buzzes and I see that it's my mother. I'm afraid to see what has happened now.

I put the phone to my ear. "I got a call from Sophie's school," she says. "She didn't show up for class."

"I walked her there," I say, but I didn't actually watch her go in. Her bestie, Ro, was waiting for her outside the school, and I assumed they went in together.

"No worries," I tell my mother. "I handle."

"I'll come in to help Baachan—"

"Nah, you rest. I'm with da gang. I go figure someting out." I end the call and put my head back on the table.

"Whassup?" Kelly asks.

"Now Sophie's missing. She didn't go to school. I have to find her."

"Maybe Pekelo can help?" Court says while still focusing on the laptop screen.

"He's still out," Kelly says. "Went ova to do someting

with the Reserves. Said he'd be back later this afternoon."

"I have to find someone to help Baachan at the shack. Sammie still in class."

"I go do," Court says. "No special orders today. Mom and Dad can handle the walk-ins." Court's parents were older; they had, in fact, adopted her in their early fifties. I don't think they would be able to keep the flower shop open without Court being in the driver's seat.

I mouth "mahalo" and Court nods.

You'd think that we'd have less customers because of Luke's murder, but its notoriety brought in a new set of curious customers who came to take selfies of themselves with a shave ice in front of our sign. There was even a hashtag #lukehightowermurderspot on Instagram that was trending on Kaua'i. I was really starting to lose hope in humankind.

I get into the Ford. A familiar weight presses down on my chest and tightens around my neck. Why am I getting a panic attack now? Not when I discovered Luke on the floor of Santiago's, and not when my father was arrested, and not at his arraignment? I sit still in the driver's seat and take two deep breaths, the calming technique I learned from Travis, who learned it from his mother.

Luckily, Waimea Middle School is just around the corner, and I don't have to travel too far. It's the same school that I attended, and I don't have the best memories. My mind couldn't focus on books and paper; I was always looking out the window, envious of the seabirds and bugs flying around so free.

Many of the office people were working there when I was going to school and let me in on campus without reservations. Nobody worries about school shootings here on

Kaua'i. That's a Mainland problem, or maybe even a Honolulu one. Not here in Waimea.

Sophie's teacher, Mrs. Ikkanda, who was my teacher as
well, stands on the playground, a whistle around her neck.
It's recess, and she scans students running around until her
gaze refocuses on me. She seems embarrassed to see me. Or
maybe embarrassed for me.

"No sign of Sophie?" she asks.

I shake my head. "Do you have any idea why she didn't
show up?"

"She's been upset about your dad, of course. She was
asking me about 'circumstantial evidence.'"

Ohmylord. Out of the corner of my eye, I see a thin
figure leaning against the chain-link fence. It's Sophie's
BFF, Ro.

I excuse myself and go over to Ro. "Howzit."

She nods, just a little. She's all skin and bones. We
know that Sophie has been sharing half of her lunch with
Ro; Mom makes sure to pack four onigiri instead of two.

"Sophie's gone missin'."

Ro doesn't respond. She's definitely not surprised.

"Did someting happen dis mornin'?"

Ro slowly opens up. Some of the other kids came
around and showed them a Facebook Live video. It was of
the beautiful Celia Johnson, claiming that our father was a
killer.

Whatthehell. I hate social media and try to stay off of
it for reasons like this.

"Do you have any idea where Sophie could have gone?"

"She was plenty huhu."

It was no surprise that Sophie was pissed off. She's not
the type to hide when she feels wronged. She faces her ene-

mies straight on. Which means she probably went to Bamboo Royal to confront Celia.

I have no idea how she would get up there with no money. But Sophie can be very persuasive. And she also had an usually large thumb, which she undoubtedly used to hitch a ride, or maybe multiple rides, to the North Shore.

I thank Ro and wish I had rice balls to give her, but all I have is a smile.

I get back in the Ford and drive as fast as I can, mindful that getting pulled over for speeding wouldn't be my smartest move, in light of my father's arrest. Driving, though, actually makes me feel better. As if I am actually accomplishing something to change our circumstances.

I make it over to Bamboo Royal in record time. It's even more beautiful in the morning light, but after I park and get out of the car, I feel a weird coolness in the breeze. The radio announcer had mentioned something about a storm reaching the island tomorrow.

Nobody is downstairs, but through the full-length windows in the back, I see Celia in a bikini sunning herself next to a pristine rectangular swimming pool. In the distance is a thicket of bamboo, probably inspiring the name of the estate.

There's an open sliding-glass door that leads outside. "So this is what a girlfriend in mourning looks like," I say when I'm a few feet away from her.

Celia turns, her wavy golden-streaked hair bouncing over her tanned shoulders. "What are you doing here?"

"I'm looking for my sister."

Celia pulls a white towel around her exposed body and tucks it around her breastbone. "Why would she be here?"

"To get your cheating ass to stop putting things up on

social media. You didn't care about Luke." Luke, in fact, sought a stranger, Sammie, to talk about Celia's infidelities. If only he had had an opportunity to have that conversation with Sammie, he might be alive right now.

Celia's eyes widen and her mouth twists into a sneer. She shoots out words like flying daggers. "You bitch."

"You the bitch."

Like a roaring tiger, she comes after me. I dodge her and slide my right ankle in back of her feet, causing her to lose her balance. The rest goes slow motion—the flailing arms and hands as she falls back-first into the pool with a big splash. I guess those early years of Dad forcing me to go to judo classes are finally good for something.

Rex and Nori, holding a joint, appear on the back deck. "What the hell—" Rex says.

"Get her out of here." Celia's wet hair sticks to her head, making her look like a pissed-off seal. Her white towel is soaked, and she frees it from her body as she walks up the pool stairs to the deck. Her tight butt is hardly covered in her thread of a bikini bottom.

"Why did you post that live feed about my father being arrested for Luke's death?" I'm not going to give up so easily.

"Because it is fact."

"You cryin' about your boyfriend but don't show up at the arraignment."

"That would have been too much for me." She puts her dripping head down in mock distress. *You ain't foolin' anyone, honey.*

"Yeah, right," I say, and she bares her perfect white teeth at me.

"Uh, Celia, why don't you pack or something?" Rex

suggests, handing her a fresh white towel.

Celia hesitates but accepts the towel and flips me off before finally going inside. *Nice. Showing your true color, sistah.*

Rex seems nonplussed by Celia's actions, as if she's like this all the time. "So are you guys leaving?" I ask.

"Hoping to. There's no reason for us to be here now."

"You and Celia are pretty tight."

"What?"

"Traveling together."

"Nori's with us, too." Rex frowns, a line deepens over the bridge of his nose. "I don't mess around with my best friend's girlfriend. Especially when he's dead."

Best friend? *Really?* I think. Wouldn't a best friend be at the arraignment as well? I don't get surfer culture, obviously. I know that my father would say the ocean is his best friend. It's always there for him, and he for it. But the ocean is powerful and doesn't have favorites. He told me once that you can only trust the sea, but I thought at the time that it could as easily kill you as bring you back to shore.

I have nothing more to say to Rex. I walk back into the house and through the front door back to my car. I hear rustling and a familiar high-pitched voice coming from the wild sugarcane field on the other side of the dirt parking lot. The grass is about ten feet tall with white fluffy tops. I cautiously approach the grass to see where the human sound is coming from.

I push away some tall grass to reveal the person I've been looking for. "Sophie! What are you doing here?"

"I have a new friend, Jimin." She holds out a hideous-looking feral rooster, its orange and green feathers matted together. "I think he's kind of sick."

Indeed, there were white spots and scabs on the rooster's red comb. "Put him down, Sophie." *All I need is for her to contract bird flu or something like that.*

"No, he helped me, Leilani. He showed me where to hide in his hangout." She goes deeper into the grass, and I struggle to keep up with her. Finally we are in a small clearing.

I let out a big breath. "We are not taking him home. Why you wen ditch school?"

"I was going come here to talk to Luke's girlfriend. To tell her to stop spreading lies about Dad. Only I ne-vah get one chance to say anything to her. I was waiting to talk to her and this car comes around. I know that car. It's Kelly's Toyota."

"Kelly was here?"

"No, his brother, Pekelo. I thought maybe you sent him to find me. So I looked around for a place to hide, and then the rooster led me into these tall grasses. . . ."

"What was Pekelo doing here?" *Didn't Kelly say that he had to do some military business with the Reserves?*

"Yah, he was smokin' and these haole guys came. They were all serious. Talking in big words."

"Did they seem like soldiers?"

Sophie shrugs her shoulders. "They were wearing aloha shirts. One was telling him to be quiet. Quiet this, quiet that. Pretty boring."

What would Pekelo have to be quiet about? I wrap my loose hair with my index fingers. Nothing was mak-ing sense. What was drawing so many people to Bamboo Royal?

"Ah, Leilani. . . ." Sophie's eyes widen as she focuses on something behind me.

Appearing from the tall grasses is about the largest

woman I have ever seen in person. She must be almost seven feet tall, with flesh that hangs from her jaw and her underarms like slabs of porterhouse steaks. She seems like she's expanding out of her clothes, which are literally torn-up T-shirts and rags pieced together with thread and shoe-laces. (Her boobs are covered up, thank God.) Her graying hair is twisted into tight cornrows against her head and long braids down her back. She looks like a sumo wrestler who has gone jungle rogue. "You trespassin' here," she says.

"I thought this was part of Bamboo Royal."

"You tink wrong."

"Eh, sorry."

"I'm not interested in sellin'. Don't bother us anymore!" She takes a few steps forward, and I notice a long wooden staff in her right hand.

"Sophie, run!"

With the rooster under her arm, Sophie whips through the grasses while I have a harder time finding an opening. I trip and land on my okole, pain shooting down to my an-kle. I let out five f-bombs in a row and try to stand up. It's my bad foot, the one I had injured my senior year of high school volleyball.

"Leilani, you okay?"

I'm able to get up, but my ankle is sore. The giant has receded in the grasses. I'm not sure about what just hap-pened, but I'm not inclined to hang around to find out. I hop on my right foot until I reach the car. Sophie trails behind with her silly rooster. I don't have the heart or en-ergy to make her abandon the bird right at this moment. "I tink dat's the lady I saw da first time we come here," Sophie tells me.

I remember the sign about protecting the land against

outsiders. She must be connected to the movement to protect the land of native Hawaiians. "Look, Uncle Rick and Auntie Barbara not far from here. I think I can drive to their house and ice my ankle. And Auntie can take a look at the rooster."

"Jimin!" Sophie insists. I recognize the name as one of the heartthrobs of her favorite K-Pop band.

I call them and Uncle Rick answers. As I expected, the door is wide open to us.

Traffic is light up here, and it only takes me about fifteen minutes to get to their house. It's small like ours, but they've taken better care of the landscaping. Also, there are only two of them—not counting all of their animals—versus sometimes seven of us when Emily is home from law school.

Uncle Rick is out on the porch waiting for us with Duke, the Labrador. We park in the driveway and walk past their small blue SUV, which has a huge gash on its passenger side. I don't mention anything about it, because I can guess what happened.

A bag of ice is placed around my ankle, and my affected leg is elevated onto pillows on the couch in the living room. Uncle Rick knows how to take good care of me.

"Where's Auntie?" I ask.

"She comin' out. Not feelin' good these past coupla days." He sits in a wicker chair, his loyal Duke by his side. "Whatchu doin' up here?"

"Long story." I don't want to get into all the details right now in front of Sophie.

"We saw a giant woman in the hills," Sophie declares, still clutching Jimin.

"Might be some squatter. There's a lot of people livin'

off the grid."

"Well, this sistah was super off the grid," I say.

"Was she with a small woman? Looks haole?"

We shake our head.

"I think dat wahine's family owns a piece of land in the middle of dat property. It's kuleana land." Rick sits back in his chair and rubs Duke's ears.

Sophie wrinkles her nose. "What dat?"

"Land that the native Hawaiian families received back in 1850s. Since dat time, the land was passed on through da generations. Some people don't even know they own it."

"Well, if I owned land, I'd build a huge bamboo castle, maybe a hundred feet high." In her excitement, Sophie squeezes Jimin too hard, causing him to squawk.

Auntie Barbara finally appears, her face again looking pale. Besides at Cannons Beach, the last time I really saw her was for a birthday dinner that my mother had for her last month. After we exchange greetings, she says, "C'mon, Sophie, lemme look at dat bird outside by our henhouse." She leads them out the kitchen door to their expansive backyard, which houses a chicken coop and cages for some tropical birds.

Uncle Rick watches them go, an almost wistful look on his face. "She always wanted kids, you know," he murmurs. "We couldn't have any. Maybe if we did. . . ."

His adult conversation makes me uncomfortable. I always wondered why Rick and Barbara didn't have children, but I felt it wasn't my business to ask.

"Thanks for all that you've done for us," I tell him. "Gettin' Mr. Brown and all."

Rick stops petting his dog. "Mo betta if you get someone from Honolulu. Someone with experience with first-degree murder cases."

Just the mention of "murder" makes me sick to my stomach.

"Brown's specialty is DUI. He's gotten a lot of people off. He's good. But maybe not good enough for your dad's situation."

"A lawyer from Honolulu is going to cost a lot," I say. I've been trying not to think about the bail money.

"Maybe we can have a GoFundMe or someting on the internet?"

"Dad wouldn't like that." He would rather rot in jail than ask for help like that. "I'm not even sure if we can make bail. I checked on the internet, and it says usually you have to come up with ten percent. That's fifty grand."

"Wasn't that old lifeguard, Darrell something, going to help out?"

I nod. I know D-man was offering to pay out of pocket—he said it was a loan—but Mom didn't want him to.

"Uncle, so you were with Dad Saturday night."

Rick nods. "We meet right hea. Handful of folks."

"Do you remember when Dad left?"

"I told da police all dis. Around nine. He said he going back to Waimea Junction to do some work."

"But he say he was going surfing."

"I guess he wen change his mind. Your faddah changes his mind plenty."

Auntie Barbara comes back into the house. "The rooster has fowl pox," she announces. "With the right care, he'll be okay. I'm gonna show Sophie what to do—"

"We're not keepin' it," I call out in a voice loud enough for Sophie to hear from outside. I have a feeling that I'm not going to win this battle.

"Why you two no stay tonight? Make Barbara happy?" Rick suggests.

I agree and check in with Mom, who's relieved that Sophie and I are together. I don't mention anything about my ankle.

That night Auntie Barbara serves us a meal of kalua pig from her Crock-Pot and we eat it over rice. Something between her and Rick seems a little off. I can't quite put my finger on it, but it's like they are too polite with each other, as if they are strangers. I recognize this in my own parents.

"Dad loves Crock-Pot kalua pig," Sophie announces as she unabashedly raises her plate for seconds. It's like she's eating for him, too. Uncle Rick sheepishly grins while Auntie Barbara's mouth falls into a straight line. Does she somehow think he's guilty of Luke's murder?

It still feels good to be away from Waimea and the mess of our family. I feel the happiest for Sophie as I watch her play with Duke, who rewards her with sloppy kisses. For a few moments in the evening, nothing seems wrong or out of whack. Both Sophie and I are able to fall asleep way before our regular bedtimes.

In the middle of the night, I hear someone stumbling in the kitchen and the door to the hallway leading to Uncle Rick and Auntie Barbara's bedroom closes. Sophie's still sleeping soundly in a sleeping bag on the floor; it would take a jackhammer two feet away to wake her up. I slowly pull myself up with my elbows and gingerly place my feet on the carpet.

My ankle's still sore, but the swelling has gone down. I limp over to the sink to get a drink of water. As I fill up a glass, I smell alcohol coming from the drain. I take a long sip and look around the small open kitchen, which is not fancy but spotless. I open the trash can with a foot pedal, but there are only plastic wrappers, soiled paper towels, and junk mail in there.

The door of the broom closet is halfway open, and I go to close it but smell some alcohol again. I check out the closet and discover what I've suspected. Sitting in a bucket, right on top of a soiled mop, is an empty bottle of vodka. So much for Uncle Rick's recovery.

Chapter Seven

WE GET UP REALLY EARLY in the morning, which isn't hard in the Chen household because of all their chickens and roosters in the back. Auntie Barbara has washed our clothes for us, and we get out of Uncle Rick's old T-shirts that we slept in. My ankle feels a bit stiff, but it's about seventy-five percent better. Both Sophie and I drink some hot coffee—I put extra cream and sugar in her travel mug—and we hug Auntie Barbara and Duke goodbye.

Outside the wind shakes the old pane windows. "Good thing you goin' before the storm," Auntie Barbara says as she pulls up her hood to go collect some fresh eggs from her chickens. "Wish your uncle could see you off, but he's not much of a mornin' person." I figure that I know what's really ailing Uncle Rick.

A few drops hit my windshield as I get back on the highway. The sky on the North Shore is gray and the palm trees bend in the wind. It's like the storm is chasing us, because it's supposed to hit the north first and then head south.

Despite the rain, I get Sophie to school earlier than usual, and she doesn't want to get out of the car and leave Jimin. The baka bird has left green globs of poop on different spots of the backseat. Luckily I had anticipated this and spread out pages of some freebie tourist magazine, but I forgot about the floor.

"Sophie, just get out and go. The rain's gettin' worse."
I make a note that I need to get new windshield wipers, as
these are cracked and jumpy. "I take care of Jimin."

She looks at me suspiciously. She knows me too well.
"You promise."

"Promise."

"Promise on Grandpop's grave?"

"Sophie!"

Clutching the plastic bag of kalua pork sandwiches that
Auntie Barbara made her, she finally opens the door. Ro,
completely soaked, is waiting for her outside. I watch both
of them run inside the school. Business is going to be lousy
today. I'm sure Baachan and Mom can pretty much handle
the late-morning crowd, which I estimate to be maybe two
or three Rainbow shave ice. This will give me time to go by
the Kauai Community Correctional Facility, back north off
of the highway, right next to a beachside golf course.

I already have called in my name to be on the visitation
list. I've been through this one time before. No one except
maybe Toma knows of my dalliance with an older guy one
summer after my sophomore year of college. Yah, this guy
used to be with a surf gang back in the day. Before it got hot
and heavy between us, he got into a fight at the Infinities
with a teenager from New York. He got locked up, and I
was questioned because I was on the beach. I visited him
once in jail, but that one time was too much, and luckily, I
had to leave the island to go back to college.

So I'm not a jail virgin; I know the drill. As the rain
pounds the Ford, I leave my necklace and money in the
glove compartment. Bring my driver's license. Know my car
license number. I hope my Crocs can pass muster.

I hear the commotion in the backseat. Jimin. What the

hell am I going to do with him? I line the car floor with a few more sheets of the magazine. With the rain coming down so hard, maybe none of the guards will notice.

I make sure that I lock my car, and I run out toward the jail's front door. I am pelted with the rain, which is practically coming down horizontally. The top of my T-shirt is wet and my bare feet squish in my Crocs. At least I'm allowed in wearing them. That's all that matters.

After I fill out forms and go through metal detectors, I sit and wait for Dad. It's not long before he appears across from me, on the other side of the plexiglass. He's wearing a bright orange jumpsuit like the other inmates, and I feel my anxiety level rising.

His beard is fully grown now, patches of white on his cheeks and brown nubs on his chin. His wild hair is almost in a mini Afro; there's no doubt where I got my hair from.

"We're working to get you out," I tell him.

"Leave me in here." He doesn't look me in the eyes.

I explain how D-man is trying to scrape together enough money to post bail.

"Leave me in here," Dad repeats. "And forget about a bail bondsman."

Well, we aren't going to listen to him, so this conversation is going nowhere. But I have some other questions for him. He shuts down. He doesn't want to answer.

"C'mon, Dad. Did Luke say anyting about Celia? How they gettin' along?"

He examines his dirty fingernails. "She had a hold on him. Nevah trusted her."

"He was talkin' to Sammie about how Celia was cheatin' on him." I explain that's why Luke went to Santiago's that night. "You have any idea who?"

Dad frowns and shakes his head. This piece of information is new to him.

"He and Rex nevah got along," he finally says.

"Really? According to Rex, they're best buddies."

Dad lets out a laugh. "Rex got no friends."

"He's goin' back to Honolulu."

"Good for him." He purses his lips. "Luke and Rex were competitors. That's how the best surfers are. No friendship out in the waves." And then as if he was recalling something painful, "Wynn Hightower even sponsored Rex instead of his own son. Said it would make Luke stronger not to have handouts from da family."

Because I know our time is short, I get right to my last question. "Why you tell Uncle Rick dat you going back to Waimea Junction?"

"Dat was my plan. Get one surfboard ready to sell. But then I saw the waves and I no can resist."

That part actually sounds completely believable. One thing my father can't say no to is a good wave.

Our fifteen minutes are over. Dad gets up. "Tell your mom no come here," he says. "I no like her see me like dis."

I'm back in the Ford and it smells something awful. I can't open the window because of the rain. Jimin now has claimed the front passenger seat.

I check my phone for Lihue Airport, and it's as I suspected. All the flights are delayed, delayed, delayed. *You're not gettin' out of Kaua'i that fast*, I think.

The rain is still heavy and a crowd is waiting underneath the airport's open-air canopy. There's little chance that I'll find Rex in this mess. But in a long line snaking from the Hawaiian Airlines counter, I spot a familiar little snot carrying a black surfboard travel bag. I get lucky; a car is just leaving a parking spot and I'm able to quickly slip in. Abandoning Jimin again, I run to the canopy to find Nori.

"Hey—" He's moved farther up in the line and is now about five people away from the counter.

"Ah, Wan-Wan-chan," Nori greets me. He's such an asshole. "What's wrong with your foot?"

I'm shocked that he noticed my injury, as I don't think I'm limping. The sixth sense of an athlete, I guess. "Nothing. Where's Rex?"

"Celia and Mr. Hightower made him stay."

The line moves a little as the airline employees call the next people forward.

The mention of Luke's father immediately catches my attention. "Mr. Hightower, what does he have to do with this?"

"His company owns Bamboo Royal. Big meeting to-morrow."

I had no idea that Mr. Hightower had a financial stake in Bamboo Royal. And what is this big meeting? It doesn't make sense that he'll be conducting business so soon after his son was found dead.

Nori moves forward in line and I move with him.

"What about Luke?" I ask.

"We have paddle-out in two weeks for him. In San Clemente. His hometown." His voice catches a little, and I detect some wetness in the corners of his eyes. Maybe this weed-smoking surfer has a heart after all.

I have gone to my share of paddle-outs, a type of surf-ing funeral tradition, in Pakala and Hanalei bays. Surfers

go out on their boards and form a circle in the still waters.
Each person says a little something in memory of the de-
ceased. I've never been in the inner circle, but have bounced
in the water on my boogie board outside of it.

It makes sense that instead of a conventional service,
Luke will have one of those. Older folks and those who
can't get in the water are usually ferried out in boats.

"So you're going to that?"

"*Mochiron*," Nori says, moving forward with his surfboard travel bag. He's now at the front of the line. "Of
course. Luke was my best friend. You want info?"

Why not, I think, although I'm sure I'm probably one
of the last people the Hightowers want to see at their son's
funeral. While we are exchanging phone digits, a uniformed airlines employee waves him over. Nori is next, and
my conversation with him is over.

I drive home in a daze. The farther west I drive, the less
wet it is, but the skies are still gray and foreboding. Once I
get home, I run to get some disposable plastic gloves and
empty the car of the yucky soiled magazine papers. I generously squirt Febreze on the carpet floor. The Ford is under
the carport, and I leave some of the windows open to clear
the air.

Jimin struts around the carport like he's in charge of
the Santiago household. I think my mom will accept him,
but Baachan? I'm sure she'll threaten to cut his head off as
she did to the chickens of her youth. I tuck him underneath
my arm like a football and take him into our backyard. If he
wants to flee, he can manage a way, but I give him some of

Auntie Barbara's chicken feed to entice him to stay, at least for Sophie's sake.

The house is completely empty, and I relish the silence. I lie back on the couch and think about my conversation with Nori. So Mr. Hightower has a company that owns Bamboo Royal. *And what other property?* I wonder. I check my phone again and Google his full name, "Wynn Hightower," and "Kaua'i." What comes up immediately, of course, is Luke's death. There's his beautiful head shot, his blond hair tousled against the background of the blue ocean and sky. I hadn't noticed before that he had a small scar on his forehead. Dad is mentioned in most of the recent stories. "Local Man Arrested in Pro Surfer's Murder." It says nothing about this local man being a mentor to the surfer, that he may even have considered him to be his son. I keep scrolling down from one page to another. It's all stories related to Luke. I add "real estate" and, sure enough, Hightower Properties comes up. They are planning a multimillion-dollar project in Moloa'a Valley surrounding Bamboo Royal. A reception and presentation to interested investors will be held tomorrow in Po'ipū.

I'm sure some people won't be happy about all that new development. Kaua'i—well, all of Hawai'i, for that matter—has been a battleground over outsiders buying up land. Would someone be mad enough about it to kill Mr. Hightower's golden son? It's definitely possible.

My phone dings with a text. It's Travis. And another ding. Emily. I feel resentful that I'm the one who has to keep everyone in the loop. I know how stupid this sounds because Travis is my boyfriend, after all, and Emily is my wingwoman sister. But the thing is, Travis doesn't know my family and Emily isn't here to help me. Making sure that they know what's going on doesn't make me feel better. It's just one more thing that I have to do. I ignore the texts for now and get back in my Crocs to walk back to Waimea Junction. I pull down a sweatshirt from a hook on the door and tighten the hood over my head.

Before I go into Santiago's, I spy Pekelo under the cover of Killer Wave's worn awning. He's smoking, and after we howzit each other, he offers me a cigarette. Of course I accept.

After a second puff, I find the guts to be direct with him. "Sophie saw you, you know. Over in Bamboo Royal."

"What, she spying on me?"

"No, brah. She was there to talk to Celia Johnson, Luke's girlfriend. She saw you there instead." I stare into Pekelo's dark eyes, measuring any differences in the speed he blinks.

He coolly blows out smoke. "I have some buddies working over there. Just looking for some work. I can't be working part-time here for too long."

Do I believe him? I so want to. I can't forget how furiously he cleaned the shack's floor of all of Luke's blood. But was he doing it for another reason other than being a good friend?

He tosses the rest of his cigarette into the rain, which is now more like a steady drizzle. "Gotta go." He gets on his bicycle. " 'K den," he says before pedaling away in the red mud.

Through the open door of Killer Wave, I see Kelly standing at the counter, nodding for me to come inside. When I do, I see that D-man is also in there, sitting barefoot on the wooden floor.

"You talk some sense in him?" Kelly asks.

I'm assuming that he is talking about his older brother. "What?"

"He's talking about maybe reenlisting in Army."

"I thought he hated it ova there."

"Hates it more here." Maybe the Army, at least, introduced Pekelo to a world of possibilities beyond the Islands.

"What you do to your ankle?" D-man asks. He's wearing sunglasses despite the rain. I swear these surfers have a sixth sense of body mechanics.

"The bum one again?" Kelly, who was the team manager of our girls' volleyball team, had been at the game when I hurt my ankle.

"It's fine."

D-man gets up from the floor. "I'm trying to get you the fifty grand. I think I can manage thirty for sure."

"D-man, there's no way Dad is going to accept that from you." I've always sensed a rivalry between the two, especially when it came to Mom. "Maybe jail is the best place for him right now. Just to cool out."

"Tommy's not gonna be able to stay locked up for long. He'll go stir-crazy." D-man knows my dad too well. He raises his palm and leaves. I suspect that he's probably going to check on Mom next door.

"I'll be right there," I call out to him as he walks out the door toward Santiago's.

"Come." Kelly pulls out a high stool from behind the counter and gestures for me to sit down. "You know that I was Coach Kawakami's best assistant physical therapist."

I grudgingly pull myself up on the stool and allow Kelly to pull the Croc from my left foot. His callused hands feel different from Travis's slender, delicate ones. I'm glad that I recently clipped my toenails. I'm not known to be well groomed, but even for me, thick toenails with crud is totally uji.

Kelly presses down on my anklebone and turns my foot slightly to the left and the right. "You'll live," he says.

"I knew dat." I ask for my Croc and slip it back on my foot.

"All kine trouble since you've been back," he says.

"We may have to find a new lawyer. One from Honolulu. This local one ain't gonna cut it, I think." I had already looked into a public defender, and despite my dad's money problems, he's still clearing too much money to be assigned one.

"Maybe you can ask Mr. Yamagishi for help." Mr. Don Yamagishi was our high school principal and former civics teacher.

"It's not so much finding one. It's the money."

"Can't you pay them at the end? If they get your dad off?"

I shake my head. "It's not slip-and-fall. They get their money up front. That's why criminal lawyers are swimming in the dough."

"Sorry, Leilani. Wish I could help, money-wise." Kelly and Pekelo are living in their late parents' old house, which still hasn't been paid off.

"We can do a second mortgage on our house. I mean, Baachan's house, because it's in her name." Grandpop Santiago, or Jiichan, had bought our small bungalow shortly after he returned from the Korean War. Both he and Baachan had been Waimea plantation kids and known each other since they were in their teens.

"Don't do it. The land is everyting. That's what Pekelo told me from small-kid time."

"What about family, Kelly? Isn't dat worth more than the land?"

Just then I see the outline of someone standing in the open doorway to the store. I squint; it's a short person. My grandmother in her muumuu.

"Do it," she says, her hand on her weak hip. "Mortgage da house."

Chapter Eight

"I think I'm bad luck," I say to Travis on the phone the next day. "I come back to help the family business, and now it looks like we may lose our house."

"How is finding a dead guy in your shaved ice business your fault?"

"It's *shave* ice, Travis."

"That's what I said."

"No, it's without—" *Forget it, who in the hell cares about that now.*

"Maybe it's time for you to move back here."

I can't even believe Travis is saying that. Abandon my whole family when things are completely falling apart? "That's not going to happen. Not for a very long time."

"When am I going to see you, Leilani? I miss you."

"I don't know. I can't think about that right now." I immediately feel bad about how awful I sound. "Listen, I have to go. I'm waiting for a call from the bank."

"Keep me posted."

"'Kay." I try to sound enthusiastic about communicating with him, when I'm actually feeling blech. *Please give me some space, people!*

I do finally get a call from the bank, and Baachan and I drive several blocks down to the Waimea branch. The sun is shining, and only the loose palm fronds by the side of the highway are signs of yesterday's storm. There are forms for Baachan to sign—she holds her pen tightly and writes slowly, as though she's tracing her signature—and then like magic, we have a line of credit. Only thing is, if we don't meet the monthly payments, we lose the house. I have no idea how we're going to get the money to repay the bank; I may have to go back to Seattle to work, live in a tent, and send money home.

During our six-block drive home, Baachan holds her purse shut, as if someone is going to be grabbing its contents. "Your Jiichan wen work so hard for dat house. All his military pay and everyting."

You didn't have to do it, I want to say to her. But that would be a lie. There's no other alternative for the Santiagos.

"Your Papa sold dat surfboard for your Mama's medicine. He won't say it, but I know." I'm shocked to hear that, but it makes sense. I've been making Cobra payments on my own medical insurance and not really thinking about my parents' situation or my little sisters'.

When Baachan gets home, she starts rummaging in the kitchen, rearranging our mixing bowls, cleaning our cracked-tile counters. We hear some crowing in the backyard, a few feet away.

"What dat?"

Sophie comes into the kitchen. "That's Jimin, Baachan," she explains.

"What dat Jimin?"

"It's her rooster. From the North Shore." I sit at the kitchen table with my bare feet on one of the chairs. My sore ankle is starting to smart, and I've placed a bag of frozen edamame on it.

"I no like one buggah rooster in *my* house."

"He's not inside the house. He's outside."

"I don't care one mile away. He's out." Baachan picks up the largest knife that we have in the house—a huge Chinese cleaver that Mama Liu loaned us that we never returned—and heads out the back door.

"No, Baachan!" Sophie shrieks, chasing her.

I cover my eyes. This is one mess I will not even try to clean up.

No rooster is slaughtered that night, though not for Baachan's lack of trying. Turns out, Jimin is actually smarter than he looks and expertly dodges Baachan's cleaver hacks.

We do have a bird for dinner that night, but it's one from the poultry section of Big Save Market. Mom makes her signature chicken long rice, a gingery soup with clear cellophane noodles. All five of us are quiet around the table, elbow to elbow, as we slurp and swallow.

After dinner, the girls go off to watch a samurai movie with Baachan in her room and I help Mom wash the dishes and put them away.

I wipe a chawan bowl with a dish towel Court had embroidered with orange koi. "What did you see in him?" I ask Mom.

Her hands scrubbing another bowl in the dishwater, she turns to me, a bit lost.

"Dad."

"He was hot, for one thing." She rinses the chawan and gives it to me.

"Yuk, Mom." Mom was in college when she spent a summer on Kaua'i and fell in love. That love resulted in a surprise—me!—that fast-tracked their relationship and led

Mom to drop out of Cal State Long Beach and move here, much to her parents' objections.

"You remember watchin' your dad surf?"

I do. He looked like a superhero, Aquaman, with his wet long hair plastered down his back, his muscular legs controlling that board.

"That caught my eye. But it was his pure heart that got me."

Huh? This was unexpected.

"You've seen one oddah man with a purer heart?" Mom has spent more of her life in Kaua'i than in California, and sometimes the pidgin can't help but come out at times like these.

Well, D-man, for one, I think. But when I think about it more, D-man is dependable but not passionate. Sometimes I have no idea what he is thinking.

"Sometimes I think Dad hates me. Even after everyting I do to help."

"Leilani, no. He loves you." She shakes the excess soap from another chawan. "Just you two the same. You both rather give stink eye than a smile."

It's true that I'm not one of those naturally happy people like Court.

"Do you know that he watched every one of your volleyball games?"

"Nah-uh."

"Kelly took videos and sent them over to me to show your dad."

"No, he nevah say."

"Dad didn't want you to know. Make a fuss."

"Fo reals?" This was hard to believe.

"He's probably more Japanese than Pinoy. Got that strict

Baachan spirit in him. You just like him. So can't show off."

What Mom is saying somehow makes sense. That it's not about only me but the family. The family is part of me.

Mom stops washing and looks me straight in the eye, her dripping hands raised as if she's preparing to do some surgery. "I don't want you to sacrifice your life for us, for me. After all of this is over, and it will be over, Leilani, I want you to go back to Seattle. Be with your boyfriend and follow your dreams."

I stay quiet and put my weight on my good leg. I have no idea what my dreams could be.

I go to work the next morning and it's slower than usual. The storm probably delayed a fresh crop of tourists from arriving. I go ahead and shave myself an ice. Instead of using one of our plastic bowls, my coffee mug serves as my container. I experiment with matcha and mango syrup, Dole Whip, and a dusting of li hing mui powder. The li hing mui adds a salty zing that somehow doesn't go with the matcha green tea flavor. The search for my signature flavor continues.

As I lick the last bit of Dole Whip from my spoon, I check my cell phone. The signal is weak in the shack, but it's good enough for me to get on the internet. I find what I'm looking for: "Wynn Hightower to hold an informational meeting for investors about the Bamboo Royal Hills real estate development."

The meeting is being held in Po'ipū in the late afternoon today at one of those hotels where young couples honeymoon. *At least it's close by, on the southern part of the island*, I think. Of course, I'm planning on attending.

I figure I need to step up my wardrobe a bit, and after Sammie comes in to relieve me, I go home to check out what I have. There are my work clothes from Seattle, but when I try on the button-down blouses and slacks, they feel strange and tight-fitting. Aisus! I must have put on some pounds from Mom's good cooking. I chuck it all for a short-sleeved floral blouse and some khaki shorts. Khaki is fancy in Hawai'i, right? Instead of Crocs, plain sandals.

I drive into the self-park lot and pick up a ticket from the machine. I'm depending on Mr. Hightower to provide validation because I'm sure as hell not going to pay ten dollars for this outing.

As I walk down the walkway, bricks of red and tan designed in a geometric pattern, I straighten out my blouse. I haven't been in one of these fancy hotels in a long time. Bright green grass and planters full of hibiscus surround the property. The building itself is a modern version of Kaua'i's plantation style, with a sloped roof and majestic tall windows. Parking lot attendants in crisp white aloha shirts run to collect car keys from waiting customers. A few feet away from the covered front entrance, a couple of yogore-type folks, political protesters I sometimes see on television, squat on the sidewalk next to a stack of preprinted signs that read "Don't Take Our Land." I'm most familiar with one of them, a tall, dark, lanky bruddah in his thirties who wears a yellow bandanna around his neck. I can smell trouble, but it seems like the hotel staff is just ignoring it for now.

I step on the humongous welcome mat, and the glass doors whoosh open for little ole me. The lobby is fit for a queen. The floor is a stone mosaic featuring a giant hibiscus. Large pastel columns go from the floor to the ceiling, maybe a hundred feet high, where a skylight reveals the blueness of the sky. The people milling around range from young couples to families with strollers to middle-aged men in aloha shirts.

On the right-hand side is a sign on an easel, "Hightower Properties Reception." That's me. Beyond the sign is a hallway that leads to an open area with high windows offering a view of the hotel's spectacular outdoor landscape: waterfalls over volcanic rocks. A woman in a red suit and wearing a pink plumeria behind her ear welcomes me, provides parking validation (yay!), tells me to sign in and write my name and business on the name tag. "Leilani Santiago, Santiago Enterprises," I write, and with a glossy folder held in place under my arm, I enter the reception area. The men in aloha shirts—a couple are in full-on suits—are gathered in clumps around high cocktail tables. The waitstaff circulate platters of pupus. I don't waste time and quickly snag a grilled jumbo shrimp skewered with a toothpick and accept a small square napkin so I look like I belong.

I've been to these kinds of events in Seattle, and the heightened bullshit in the room actually gets me excited. Everyone has some kind of angle, something they want to sell or acquire. My job will be to figure out who Mr. Hightower really is.

Along the edges of the room are some long tables. "Meet Surf Champions Celia Johnson and Rex Adams" invites a foam-core board on an easel. And like real-life dolls, seated at a long table are Luke's girlfriend and one of his two BFFs.

Celia, wearing a lei of white orchids, literally sneers at me. She's Miss High Makamaka, thinking she's better than everyone. "What are you doing here?" she asks me.

Rex sits farther down from her, looking sheepish. He

seems like he wants to be anywhere but here.

"I guess you two changed your mind about leaving town," I say. I hold the sales folder against my chest.

"We meet our commitments. Because we are grown-ups." Celia raises her head, as if she, a person who gained her fame from standing on a polyurethane board in the water, is better than me.

Did anyone *really care about Luke?* I wonder. Because the only person who does is behind bars.

I nod toward the well-designed poster. "Looks like this has been in the works for a while."

Rex, who looks like a fallen Greek god with leis of ti leaves around his neck, slumps back in his chair. *Is it guilt making him so miserable?* I wonder. Either he really cared for Luke, or maybe he is responsible for his friend's demise.

A couple of gray-haired people approach the table, taking out head shots from the marketing folder and requesting that Celia and Rex sign them. It's beyond corny, and I walk over to another corner of the room and thumb through the Hightower Enterprises material. There are full-color schematics of the new development, a cascading structure with escalators, luxury condominiums, and storefronts. It looks like something that belongs in Hong Kong, not in the Moloaʻa Valley.

The PA system crackles. Wearing a baby blue aloha shirt, Wynn Hightower stands at the podium. He also has leis of ti leaves streaming down his chest. I hate to admit it, but for an old guy, he's pretty good-looking, in a George Clooney type of way.

The hotel waitstaff moves throughout the room with their trays of champagne glasses. I grab one, the bubbles still fizzing.

"I want to welcome all of you to this celebration of bringing a new project to the Garden Isle. Bamboo Royal Hills." He raises his glass in making his toast, "Kāmau kīaha." Wynn's accent isn't bad for a haole.

"Kāmau kīaha," the crowd replies back, and we all take a swig of the champagne. It's delicious. Definitely expensive.

He then goes on to say how much the new development will contribute to the island's economy. Locals will get jobs, blah, blah, blah. My eyes start to glaze over, and I concentrate on enjoying the champagne.

I'm in the middle of my last sip when I smell the spicy scent of men's cologne next to me. "What are you doing here?" A smile is plastered on his face, but the tone emanating from Wynn's mouth is anything but kind.

"Checking out the new project," I say after swallowing.

"This event is for investors only."

"Maybe I'm interested in investing."

"Maybe you should be interested in figuring out how to make a living after your father is sentenced to prison indefinitely for killing my son."

"My father is innocent."

"We'll see about that. In the meantime, I'd appreciate it if you left the premises."

Hey, this is a free country, I feel like blasting him.

"She's with me," says someone in a familiar hoodie next to me. It takes me a second to register Sean Cohen's presence.

Wynn Hightower focuses on Sean's name tag and carefully measures his worth, in contrast to the speed with which he dismisses mine. "Well, watch her, then," he says. "Make sure she doesn't cause any trouble." With that, Wynn dips his head and makes his way to his more moneyed guests.

What a jerk! Anger surges through my body. "What

are you doin' here?" I ask Sean.

"I was curious. Wanted to hear the presentation."

I take a look at his name tag. Underneath Sean Cohen, it states "SC Enterprises."

I know that company. I've been writing our Waimea Junction rent checks to that company. SC Enterprises is our landlord.

Sean follows my eyes, and his face, and even his ears, become flushed.

"I can explain—"

SC. Sean Cohen. "Why didn't you tell me that you owned Waimea Junction?"

"I was planning to. I just didn't want you to get the wrong idea."

"Are you part of this? What these assholes are selling? And do you know him, Wynn Hightower?" I think back to the police station when we were picking up my father. Was Sean faking that he didn't know Luke's father?

"No, never met him in person until today. But we know of each other."

"Because you rich white guys all belong to the same club, right? And what's this, 'Make sure that she doesn't cause trouble.' Like you own me or something."

"He said it, not me."

"But you're after the same things? You probably want to make Waimea Junction a Waimea Royal."

"No, of course not. I mean, it could use some upkeep and a fresh coat of paint."

"I thought so! And what was it about making soap? Just a stupid lie." I shake my head. I can't believe this. Dad's in jail, our house is mortgaged, and now we may lose both Santiago's and Killer Wave. I'm starting to get one of my panic attacks. I need fresh air to breathe.

I rush out of the reception, accidentally knocking someone's California roll off their paper plate. I leave my empty glass on the concierge table. The shiny folder slips out of my hand, and one of the hotel's staff quickly removes it from the mosaic stone floor as if it never existed. I strip off my name tag and pluck it off my fingers.

Finally I'm outside, but it's complete chaos.

"Don't take our land!" "Don't take our land!"

The two protesting bruddahs have multiplied into at least thirty folks, all carrying signs and chanting around the sidewalk and spilling out into the street and also near the parking attendants. The police are here, and officers are standing around the perimeter of the hotel.

Joining the protesters is the giant woman we saw in the fallow sugarcane fields. I don't think she recognizes me because she hands me a sign as I get close. Holding that placard makes me feel powerful, like I have a tool that will help me get heard.

"Leilani! Leilani—" I hear a man's voice calling out to me.

"Leave me alone, Sean!" I scream back, hoping the protesters will prevent him from approaching me.

"Don't take our land!" "Don't take our land!"

But he keeps walking forward, that stupid name tag still affixed to his hoodie.

I'm sick of this. All of this. Why do outsiders feel that they can come here and disrupt our lives?

With both hands I hold the sign above my head. "Don't take our land! Don't take our land!" I yell at him at the top of my lungs, causing him to take some steps back, into the brick loading zone. I don't know if his sneaker got caught on the brick, but before I know it, he has stumbled and fallen on his okole.

Wynn Hightower has burst through the crowd of on-lookers and patrolling police officers. "I want this woman to be arrested." He points his finger at me, an arrow aimed straight at my heart. "She's disturbing the peace."

A couple of police officers, including Andy Mabalot, have now come next to us, ready to intervene.

"Really, Andy?" I say to him.

"You're on his property."

"This is not Bamboo Royal."

"I own this hotel, too," Wynn says. Of course.

We can't let this keep happening. "Don't take our land," I chant, sticking the sign in his face, so close that it touches his forehead.

"Get her out of here," he directs Andy. Andy's face hardens as he pulls my hands behind my back, causing the poster to fly onto the ground, and secures plastic ties to my wrists. The plastic cuts into my skin and I tell myself not to cry. Andy and another police officer lead me to one of the squad cars.

"You let her go!" The giant woman steps forward onto Wynn Hightower's property. As I am pushed into the backseat, I watch as five officers take her down. A smaller woman tries to defend her, and she also is taken into custody. "Don't take our land! Don't take our *land!*" The crowd is getting louder. Bits of trash—smashed fast food cups and napkins—are now being thrown onto the hotel's driveway and pristine grass landscape.

"I'll get you out," Sean, his glasses crooked on his face, calls out to me through the open window of the moving police car.

Now I feel exactly like Dad. *Just leave me alone.*

Chapter Nine

I wish I could say that I don't know what it's like to be riding in the backseat of a police car, but I'd be lying. During my senior year of high school, there was an "incident." It involved another student who happened to be stalking Emily, who was a junior at the time. Kirk would be waiting for her every day when she was dismissed from her last class. He would follow about five yards behind, stop where she stopped, and even wait for her to emerge from a friend's house. Later I would discover that Kirk was neglected and sometimes abused at home, but I still wouldn't have done anything different. Mom had spoken to our high school counselor, but since what Kirk was doing was outside of school grounds, there was little they could do. As he was a minor, only sixteen, the police didn't want to get involved. Mom went to his home to talk to his mother, but she defended her son, saying we were lying, crazy Filipinos.

So I had to take things into my own hands, right? Those hands took hold of the shoulders of the military jacket that Kirk was wearing and slammed his back into a chain-link fence at our school. I verbally beat him up, threatening every act of bodily harm that I could imagine if he continued his stalking ways. Court was begging me to stop, but I didn't listen to her until Mr. Yamagishi pulled me off of Kirk. Right behind him was Kirk's mother, who had been watching the whole time.

Mr. Yamagishi tried to calm the mother down, but she insisted on calling the police. It must have been a slow day at the Kaua'i police station because lo and behold, who should show up but Dennis Toma, who was a lieutenant at the time. They didn't lead me out with my hands in plastic ties that day, but I did get a chauffeured ride in the back of a police car. I had just turned eighteen, and I guess was technically an adult. I was taken in for questioning, perhaps to appease Kirk's mother.

I was never charged with any crime, but I was marked as a troublemaker at the Kaua'i police department. Marked as a girl who was out of control, a local vigilante. Toma gave me a good talking-to, told me that I needed to break my family's rebellious cycle. I had no idea at the time what he was talking about.

I was close to getting expelled, but as it turned out after the "incident," all these girls from my high school came forward. Kirk stalked them, too, and on top of that, left morbid notes in their lockers. Each one of them was scared to come forward until they saw me confronting him on school grounds. Mr. Yamagishi worked it out with the principal, and I had to serve detention for three months, but there was nothing on my school record that would have affected my acceptance to UW. And Kirk was transferred out of our school; I never knew what happened to him afterward.

Today is a different story, as I'm officially booked. They have taken my fingerprints and my mug shot. At least I'm wearing my flowered blouse and a bit of makeup, so I guess I dressed up for the occasion. "I want my phone call," I tell

Andy in my best *Law & Order* voice, and I'm handed a receiver. Who can I call who won't freak out?

D-man picks up on the second ring.

"It's me, Leilani. I've gotten in some trouble."

"Lihue Police Station?" The location must have shown up on his phone. He tells me he's on his way.

When that's finished, Andy takes me to a line of small individual cells, all empty. He opens the door on the far holding cell and I walk in. The gate of bars clangs closed. Andy is now dead to me.

I sit down on the skinniest mattress ever, which rests on top of a metal bedpan. I smell bleach that's been applied to get rid of the scent of piss. Guess what, it doesn't work. Right next to the bed is a miserable stainless steel toilet. I tell myself that I will not use that benjo, no matter what. I'll soil my shorts before I lower them in a jail cell.

More voices, both female and male, footsteps, and the clanging of more jail doors. As there are walls that divide each cell, I can't see who has been locked up next to me.

Breathe, Leilani, breathe. My anxiety is going up again. I close my eyes. To avoid the piss smell, I try to not breathe out of my nose and inhale through my mouth instead. The relaxation technique doesn't work as well that way.

I try instead to think about how we are going to clear my dad. By now the police must have found something on Luke's phone. Toma must have interrogated Celia. Maybe whoever was having an affair with Celia decided to finish Luke off. I can't imagine someone being so captivated by her to kill, but some folks, especially obsessed men, can be lolo and unpredictable.

I lie back on the bed and wince. The surface is even harder than the ground. I won't be staying here overnight, right? I imagine my father being in here a few days ago and now at the real jail, the correctional center. This whole thing is so wrong. When Kelly gets religious on me, which is not that often, he talks about the truth setting us free. Where is our truth? I don't see it, God.

I think I hear a trumpet blowing. A few beats and again. "What the heck?" I say out loud.

I hear some chuckling in the next cell. "That's Patsy. My girlfriend. Her snores are legendary, can be heard as far as the Big Island, I'm told. At least she's getting some rest," a woman, most likely middle-aged, says. The voice is not a local one. My guess is that she isn't from Hawai'i.

"Are you from the protest at the hotel in Po'ipū?" I ask.

"Were you the first one to get arrested? We saw the police taking you away and Patsy went nuts."

"Is she kind of tall?" I try to be as diplomatic as possible.

"Seven feet of heaven."

"Eh, I think my sister and I may have seen her before. In Moloa'a Valley."

"That's where my land is. From my great-grandmother. It's not even an acre. Found out about it recently. Through a quiet title lawsuit."

"What's a quiet title?"

"Hightower sued a bunch of us to clear the title of some kuleana land. Land that the natives like my great-grandmother owned. To tell you the truth, I didn't even know about it. But I wanted to check it out before I agreed to sell it. Turns out that I didn't want to let it go." Here I thought that the giant woman was the one with ties to the land. "We came from LA. Patsy is a character actress and is going for some roles with *Hawaii Five-0*. She's kind of gone Method with the outfit, hair and all. But that's just how she approaches her roles."

"She chased me and my sister off of your land. I think she was holding a spear."

"Oh, sorry. She can go overboard."

Quiet. Sophie had said something about some men saying "quiet" to Pekelo. Could it be that the Kahuakai boys had a claim to kuleana land, too? "Do you know how many families are involved?"

"Dozens. Our ancestors were all part of the Hawaiian system, charged with taking care of the land and taking care of each other. When the land-tenure system changed into divvying up private property, the maka'āinana, the common laborers, were given a portion of the land they tended. We're just claiming what was given to them."

All this was covered in my Hawaiian Studies classes in high school. I paid enough attention to get decent grades at the time, but once I left Kaua'i, all history involving the maka'āinana left my consciousness.

Footsteps again. Andy appears with a key in hand. "Leilani, you got bailed out." He speaks softly, but that nice-guy routine isn't going to work on me. He opens the door, and I silently thank D-man. He has come through for me again.

The woman who'd been talking to me pokes her arms out in between the bars of her cell door. Her arms are covered in fine red hair and she has age spots on the back of her hands. "Lucky girl," she says to me as I pass.

"Good luck," I respond.

In the next cell over, Patsy the actress is still fast asleep. Only three-quarters of her body fit on the uncomfortable bed; her lower legs dangle toward the ground. I see her patchwork clothing in a new light now. It's a costume, art.

At the booking station, my jewelry, phone, wallet, and

keys are returned to me. I don't have anything to say to Andy and the other officers. The door to the booking area is open and I'm free.

I walk outside and find myself in the parking lot. The whole gang is here: D-man, Kelly, Pekelo, and Court. "Thanks for bailing me out," I say to D-man. "I hope it wasn't too expensive."

Kelly gestures to someone standing next to a white van. "He beat us to it."

Sean stands awkwardly by a concrete parking bumper. At least he has taken off his name tag.

I shake my head. If only they knew that this guy is probably going to dismantle Waimea Junction as we know it? "I'll pay you back. Every single penny," I say without looking at his face.

"I told them, Leilani," Sean says. "I told them that I'm the new owner of Waimea Junction. But I don't have any plans to kick anyone out or raise the rents. I do want to make some improvements."

"Our building could use some help. Right now it's kinda hammajang," Pekelo says, and I glare at him like he's a traitor. That reminds me that we need to have another conversation about what he was really doing at Bamboo Royal.

D-man volunteers to drive me home, but I need to pick up my car from the self-parking lot at the hotel in Po'ipū.

"I go get'um," Kelly says, and I gratefully give him my keys and the parking ticket. As I get into D-man's old pickup truck, I'm so thankful for my crew.

"I don't think he's all bad," D-man says. I know he's talking about Sean.

"Says you." I cross my arms and slump down in the passenger seat. "He could have come clean from beginning.

Why lie and say he going make soap?"

"I think he's really making soap."

"Fo' real? Whassamatta wid him?"

"Rich high-tech guy from Silicon Valley. That's what they do after they make their millions."

"Silicon Valley? He said he came from Sunnyvale."

"That's in the middle of Silicon Valley, Leilani." D-man thinks I'm clueless, which I certainly can be at times. "I don't think he's like Luke Hightower's father."

"We'll see," I tell him. I have to see with my own eyes.

When we are in front of my house, I ask D-man if he wants to come in.

He hesitates.

Sophie bounds out the door and down from the porch. "Dad's home!" she announces.

The pickup's engine is still running. D-man tells me that he has to tend the bar. Good excuse.

"Why did D-man drop you off?" Sophie asks when I approach the house.

"Eh, had some car trouble. No big deal. Kelly's going bring da Ford latah." No sense in getting the fam all worried about me, especially since Dad has returned.

The minute I enter the house, I can tell that the mood has lifted. Dani has made a banner out of construction paper, markers, and tape: "Welcome home Dad." I hear a commotion in the kitchen, which usually means Baachan is cooking. Mom is sitting on the couch with her feet up on Dad's lap.

Dad seems a little different. Like his sharp edges have been smoothed a bit. He's freshly shaved the sides of his beard and even trimmed his goatee. When Mom sees me, she gets up as if she wants me to have some private time

NAOMI HIRAHARA   123

with Dad.

"You shouldn't have put a second mortgage on the house," he says, not sternly but more deflated, resigned.

"It's in Baachan's name. She wanted to do it. I couldn't stop her." I sit cross-legged on the tan jute rug. Mom brings me a glass of mango shake made from coconut water. I guess we are celebrating tonight.

"So who got you out?"

"Mr. Brown and Rick. But I have to wear this." He points to his bare left ankle, where a black square monitoring device has been attached. "Can only be home or at Santiago's."

"We're getting you a new lawyer."

"Mr. Brown good enuff."

"No, Dad, he may be a nice man, but he's not good enough. We have to find you a hotshot lawyer in Honolulu."

Both of us are quiet for a moment and take long sips of our mango shakes. The sweet richness hits the spot. I can't believe everything that I've gone through today.

I have some nagging questions still, beginning with the swastika surfboard. "Is Baachan right? That you sold it to pay for Mom's medicine?"

Dad ignores my specific question. "Luke gave it to me. He told me he didn't want it anymore."

"But why?"

"I dunno. All of a sudden when we get off da plane. He was plenty quiet when we landed. Like he got a bad message on his phone." Dad rubs the back of his bare feet. "So he told me to take it off his hands. I know a dealer who knows how to sell anything. One call from the airport, and he says he'll come and collect it early next morning."

Apparently he did come Sunday morning around eight o'clock, unaware that Luke's cold body was inside Santiago's.

Dad still doesn't admit that Mom's health was behind the quick sale. He's got so much pride. I can only help him if he lets me know what's going on.

"Did something happen at the meeting Saturday night?"

"What meeting?"

"I know, Dad. Mom told me. You've been going to AA."

Dad grunts.

"Uncle Rick helping you out, right?"

Dad finally verbally responds. "I da one who's helpin' him out." Again my dad's pride.

"Someone's here with your car," Sophie calls out from the porch.

Someone, that's Kelly, you silly girl. I rise from the jute rug, only to see someone altogether different coming up our walkway.

"I thought Kelly was getting my car," I say to Sean as he hands me the keys.

"Come in for grindz." Mom holds open the screen door and Sean looks confused for a second. "C'mon, don't give us haoles a bad name here. Grindz, food, dinner."

It's too late to stop Mom. Sean must be hungry because he adjusts his glasses and walks in. Before he gets to the living room, I pull him aside. "Say nothing about what happened today," I hiss in his ear. He looks surprised but understands that I'm dead serious.

Usually we eat at the kitchen table, but there are too many of us. We remove Dani's art projects from the dining room table and add another table leaf to enlarge the surface. I take a rag from the sink and scrub the table of glitter and paint, or at least as much as I can manage. We bring out a roll of paper towels and a glass mug filled with pairs of hashi. Everyone grabs the chopsticks, and Dani holds out a special pink Hello Kitty pair to Sean. He smiles and accepts it. One of his lower canine teeth sticks out, and I have to admit it's pretty cute.

Baachan brings out the whole Panasonic rice cooker and puts it down in the middle of the table, and Mom brings over a stack of bowls, all mismatched. Hot white rice is scooped into the bowls, and they are passed around to each person.

My father sits at the head of the table, with Sean sitting at his right and me on the left. "So, Dad, dis Sean Cohen. Da guy who drove us in his white van. He da new owner of Waimea Junction."

"I thought he made soap." Dad speaks as if Sean's not there.

"I do, sir, or else I'm planning to. All natural sourced ingredients, no sulfates or parabens."

"What's a paraben?" asks Dani, who is shushed by Mom.

Dad finally takes a look at Sean. "So you SC Enterprises."

Sean nods. "I've now moved here permanently from California. Sunnyvale."

"That's in Silicon Valley," I say.

Baachan tosses a knit trivet in the shape of a pineapple onto the middle of the table. Then comes a huge pot of steaming goodness. "Dis okazu," she explains, shoving a ladle into the stew. "Pork. Potato. A lil bit of everyting."

Dad gestures for Sean to fill his bowl first, and he complies. He waits until every bowl is filled. "Itadakimasu," we

Santiagos call out. Sean cautiously uses his chopsticks to bring the food to his mouth, chews, and swallows. "Delicious. You'll have to teach me how to make it."

We all start laughing, even Dad. "You can't teach okazu," Baachan says. "It tells you what it's gonna be."

"But I've seen lots of okazu-ya places all over the island," Sean says.

"Oh, dat's fancy places. Not Santiagos'."

We all stop talking for a while, enjoying the meal and the mango shakes, and I feel the stress of being a jailbird melting away. After I had returned from the police station in high school, Mom told me, "Don't let this experience define you, Leilani. You aren't a bad person. You just have to learn how to deal with your anger in a different way." I guess that I still haven't learned. But I'm not going to let what happened to me today define me.

"My sistah ova dea in California," Baachan abruptly says. Her dentures have been making clicking noises, and somehow eating has made her top bridge go slightly lopsided.

I am surprised that Baachan's even talking about her blood relatives on the Mainland. Up to this point, the subject was taboo. I know she was kind of abandoned on Kaua'i with her grandparents on the plantation in the 1930s, when her parents and older sister left for greener pastures.

"Where in California?" Sean asks.

"Los Angelesy." There's no point in correcting her pronunciation.

"Have you gone to visit?"

"Nah, Los Angelesy not for me."

That Baachan shared something so personal makes our dinner more intimate. We are not Santiagos and a stranger.

We are family.

When we are finished stacking all the dirty plates and collecting the chopsticks, Dad gets up and says to Sean, "Tanks for bringing ova our car."

After dinner, Sean and I sit on tourist magazines on top of the wooden porch.

I have some fresh fruit that Mom purchased from the local farmers' market. I cut into the papaya first. I brush away the little black pellet seeds and slice the orange flesh into quarters. I offer one of them to Sean. "It's papaya."

"I know that much," he says, taking a big bite.

"Just checkin'."

After he chews, he locks his hands together. "Look, I want to apologize. I should have told you who I was. But I had a feeling it wouldn't go over well. I know how people feel about outsiders buying up the land."

I trim the papaya skin and continue listening.

"I did well in tech. Sold my company to one of the big ones. I was finished with it all. Working twenty hours a day. Literally being chained to my job. I came to Kaua'i with my girlfriend—she practically forced me to take a break—and I fell in love . . . with the island. The girlfriend and I, on the other hand, broke up. Ironic, huh?"

I don't want to get into girlfriend-boyfriend talk, because that means I would have to mention Travis and to tell you the truth, I'm not quite sure what he means to me right now.

"And since I'm coming clean with everything, I should probably tell you that I am looking into who bought that surfboard."

"How come?" This is really not his business.

"I'm curious who would want to buy something with

a swastika."

"But I thought you said the symbol meant something different before the Nazis got ahold of it."

"I know. I want to make sure."

That still seems a bit odd to me, yet I decide to let it go for now.

"I also had a long talk with all the tenants, all your friends at Waimea Junction. I want to hear what they want from the property. I'm going to have a luau tomorrow for everyone connected with Waimea Junction. A kalua pig and everything."

"You mean in an imu? You'll have to dig a hole on your property."

"Yeah, I know. Kelly and Pekelo's friend are going to take care of the cooking. They're already starting to get things ready. There will be lotta grindz."

"Really?" I start laughing at his attempts at pidgin.

"And I can help you with your father. I know some good lawyers in Honolulu. I'm sure they can recommend a top-notch criminal one."

"That would help." I now have another fruit, the size of a huge hand grenade, that is covered in spiky red leaves.

"Dragon fruit. I know that, too." Sean is feeling pretty proud of himself.

"But have you ever had a Hawaiian one?"

Sean shakes his head. "No, but I can't wait to try."

After we finish half of the dragon fruit, Sean excuses himself to make plans for the luau. He seems relieved that the truth about his identity is out.

I peel the other half of the dragon fruit in the quiet of twilight. I forgot to ask Sean about what he knows about kuleana land quiet titles. Being a privileged owner, he must have come across such things. There are other issues that Sean can't help me with. Like why would Luke just give his surfboard to Dad? What was that text message he received?

A familiar SUV, its headlights on, comes up the hill and enters our driveway.

Mama Liu is dropping someone off at our house. I squint and stand up, the skin of the dragon fruit falling from my lap. It can't be, but it is.

It's Travis.

Chapter Ten

SOMETHING IS A BIT OFF. Here I've been fantasizing about this for months, but our reunion is not what I expected.

First, his hands. They feel clammy, like octopus tentacles. Why didn't I notice that before?

When he kisses me on the lips, it feels strange. I don't get that spark of electricity, the chicken skin all over my body. The kiss feels cold, clinical, as if we are engaging in some kind of medical procedure.

Dani and Sophie have gathered in the doorway, the screen door held open by their dirty bare feet and hands. "This is like *The Bachelor*," Sophie whispers in Dani's ear, loud enough for me to hear.

I glare at them over Travis's shoulder, and they erupt in giggles, then run back into the house, the screen door slapping closed behind them.

"*The Bachelor?*" Travis grins. "I should have brought a rose."

"Ya huh," I say. He has no idea that another bachelor graced these doors just a few minutes ago.

"What are you doing here?" I try not to say that in the tone I'm thinking it in my head: *WHAT ARE YOU DOING HERE?!*

"I wanted to surprise you. I know everything seems to be crazy right now, so I wanted to take you away."

"Eh, take me away what?"

"You look like you're having a heart attack. I know you have responsibilities here and can't go far. So I booked an Airbnb a few blocks away from your house. Only it's much bigger." He might as well have added "nicer." I feel defensive for no good reason.

"Well, come in and meet the fam," I say as enthusiastically as lukewarm bathwater.

Travis leaves his duffel on the porch and smooths out his longish, wispy hair. He's wearing a plaid button-down shirt and dark skinny jeans. Back in Seattle, he would be considered geeky sexy, but here in Waimea, he looks strange.

"Hello, Santiago family," he says as he walks into the house. I don't know why he's acting so upbeat.

Mom is crocheting some pot holders and looks up over her reading glasses.

"Ah, Mom, this is Travis. Made a surprise visit."

She puts down her craft project and starts to get up, holding on to the arm of the couch for support.

"No, no, please, don't overextend yourself. Leilani told me all about it." Travis goes to her and shakes her hand. Mom looks a bit stunned.

My father walks into the living room from the bedroom hallway. "Now who dis guy?"

"Tommy, it's Leilani's boyfriend. From Seattle."

He frowns and retreats back to his bedroom.

"He's a little tired," Mom explains.

"Well, makes sense from having to go to jail and all."

Baachan's mouth falls open and her top dentures come loose. She's working on a puzzle at the kitchen table, and the last thing I'm going to do is introduce Travis to her. Was he always this awkward?

"Ah, Travis is staying—how long are you staying?"

"I could only get four days off of work." Only three nights, thank God.

I explain to Mom that Travis has already rented a nearby Airbnb and that I'll be staying there with him.

"Good," Mom says to me. "And take a few days off of work. Dad can run things at Santiago's. In fact, it's better if he has something to do."

I go into my bedroom to stuff a few pieces of clothes and underwear into a Big Save Market plastic bag. I feel a bit discombobulated. Am I happy or unhappy that my boyfriend is here in Hawai'i? After all that has happened in the past few days, I don't know how I feel about it.

Travis wanders into my bedroom. "You sleep here?" His hand is on his hip as he soaks in my beautiful décor. High school banner, photo collage of Court, Kelly, and me wearing baseball caps and doing hiphop moves, a poster of Beyoncé. "It's like a tomb. No windows."

"I like it that way. You know me and mornings."

"If I lived in Hawai'i, I'd live in a glass house. I'd let the sun in 24/7."

I've never seen Travis so rah-rah about the sun. Maybe the gray skies of Seattle had been taking a toll on him.

We look up the location of the rental on our phones. Totally walkable. We say goodbye to Mom, and I'm thankful that the girls and Baachan are behind closed doors watching their samurai movies.

"It smells so good here," he says as we walk up the dark road. Plumeria blossoms hang in bunches on expansive, rounded trees. On waxy bushes are gardenias, which glow white under the moon.

After a few blocks we pass a beautiful plantation house that's been redone. In typical plantation style, the roof is

wide, with the pitch split in two places. Eaves are supported
by double brackets. There's a single light on over the wide
porch. Otherwise, it's dark. No one seems to be home.

"Wow, I've never noticed that one before," I say. I never
go this way in my neighborhood.

"Our place is right next door."

The Airbnb is also a plantation house, more modest
than the updated one, yet still gorgeous and with a terrif-
ic view. Looking up the combination on his phone, Travis
opens the lock and pushes the door open. He gives me a
weird look, and at first I'm worried that he's going to try to
carry me across the threshold or something. Thank God, he
doesn't try anything so cheesy.

He clicks on the light. "Can you imagine living in a
house like this?"

In a way, I can't. It's so quiet and the hardwood floors
are spotless and shiny. I would be scared to walk on them.
My bag of clothing seems hopelessly out of place in such a
pristine home. We wander from room to room, oohing and
aahing about various features—the exposed-wood beams,
the clean white walls and ceiling, the pretty floral-print
couches, modern kitchen, and so on.

He takes my hand—his hands now feel warmer than
before—to go upstairs and find the master bedroom. My
plastic grocery bag of clothes and I follow.

The harsh light filters through the opaque curtains, nearly
blinding me as I try to open my eyes.

I look at the empty space next to me on the bed. Only
crumpled-up luxury sheets. Travis has already gotten up. I

haven't slept this well in a long time.

When I go downstairs in an oversize Hamura Saimin T-shirt, I find Travis beating eggs in a small bowl.

"They left a few things in the refrigerator for us. And I brought coffee." He points to the coffeemaker. This is why I love him.

Slices of bread pop up in the toaster. I grab the slices and put each on a different plate. "Umm. Raisin."

We bring everything outside onto the deck, which overlooks Waimea. Sitting at the table with steaming mugs of coffee, fluffy eggs, and toast, I feel like I'm in one of those travel advertisements—"Experience Kaua'i."

"What should we do today?" Travis asks when the food is all gone and only a bit of the coffee is left.

"We can go hiking up Waimea Canyon. I even saw some day packs here and water bottles."

"I'd totally go for that."

"I'll see if I can borrow my family's car," I tell him. I also need to find better hiking footwear than my Crocs. All the dirty plates go into the deep farmhouse-style stainless steel sink, and Travis volunteers to clean up the kitchen while I go to my family's house.

I go outside, and coming out of the neighboring house is a man with a mop of curly hair. It can't be, but then I see the white van parked in the driveway. Shit. I walk in the opposite direction, hoping that Sean hasn't noticed me.

"Leilani, is that you?"

"Ah—" I stop, closing my eyes, and turn. "Eh, mornin'."

"What are you doing here?" Sean walks down the driveway to the street.

"I'm staying in that Airbnb next door," I tell him. "My boyfriend made a surprise visit."

"I didn't know you had a boyfriend."

"Well, you know, yeah." So awkward. "So you live here?"

"Yeah, I've been working on it for a while. It's finally livable."

The house in daylight is even more impressive. "It's really beautiful. I don't really come up this way."

"You want a tour?"

I look back at the rental. Why not take a quick detour?

The house, also two stories, has a golden sheen to it. Inside, the floors and furniture look like they are made from koa wood, and Sean confirms it. I've always been partial to our native wood, the unique striping that makes the wooden surface almost three-dimensional. Upstairs, next to the master bedroom is a corner library, custom shelves built to accommodate smaller books at the top and heavy coffee-table books on the bottom. Large windows allow the eastern light to stream in. There's also a big lamp with a Tiffany glass shade next to a comfy leather easy chair.

"You read a lot."

"Yeah, I'm hoping one day to maybe have a little pop-up bookstore in Waimea Junction."

"You can call it Books and Suds."

Sean looks confused.

"You know, books and soap. Or maybe beer."

"Oh, yeah." He points at me. "I got it. I like it."

Nah, it's totally lame, but I appreciate that he doesn't tell me so.

He's quiet for a moment and studies my face as if he's trying to figure out if he can trust me. "You want to see my war room?"

I'm surprised and a little worried. *What the hell is a war room? Is he into Dungeons & Dragons? Tin soldiers? Or some-*

thing more along the lines of Fifty Shades of Grey?

I shrug my shoulders, trying to act casual, as if all people have a war room in their homes. Sean doesn't look that physically strong, so I think that I can take him if something takes a dark turn.

He opens a narrow door next to his library and flicks on the light. I'm not sure if it's a large utility closet or a baby nursery, but there are no windows. On one side he's propped up large pieces of foam core with photos of men wearing swastikas, buildings that look like prisons, and maps of Hawai'i.

Oh my God. He's created a crazy wall, an evidence board like the ones in the old *Law & Order* episodes.

"I'm a Nazi hunter," he announces, and I start wondering if he's mento or something. "One of the last Nazis is hiding out here in Hawai'i." He pushes his index finger into the face of a balding white man in a photograph. Underneath the color photo is his name: John Fischer. Sean explains that's his last known alias.

"The guy must be a hundred or so."

"That doesn't excuse what he did during World War II."

"Well, you betta catch him before he make, die, dead."

"That's my plan."

"That's why you were so into that swastika surfboard." Sean had said something like it was personal.

"The dealer emailed me late last night. He has a buyer. I'm going to follow up with him."

"It might be a rabid surfboard collector, that's all," I warn him.

"Maybe." Sean's brown eyes look different here. Laser focused and determined. He frightens me a little.

We leave the war room, and to tell you the truth, I'm not sad about it. I wonder why Sean feels so motivated to do something so intense like that, but I don't feel like we know each other well enough for me to ask.

"Well, anyway, I hope you can come for the luau. Both of you, of course. I think the pig will be ready around four."

"'K den. I'll see." I make my way down the stairs to the front door.

"Hope you'll be there."

I walk down the road, and I feel like a bit of a two-timer, at least in my heart. Is this how it first happened with Celia? That she and Luke weren't quite clicking, or maybe spending too much time apart, and she started hanging out with someone new? *I'm not a cheater, though*, I tell myself. Absolutely nothing has happened between me and Sean.

As I make my way to my family's house, I hear roosters trying to out cock-a-doodle-doo each other. The loudest one is Jimin, the new rooster on the block. I'm sure the whole neighborhood appreciates the monster we have brought in.

When I go into the house to get my hiking shoes and retrieve the car keys, I see my father sitting alone in the living room. His face is grayish; his hair, bedraggled. He winces as he massages the ankle shackled to the monitoring device. I'm reminded that this getaway with Travis is pretend. Nothing in my family is fine.

It's a good day to hike Waimea Canyon. I usually go later in the day, right before sunset, but there's a hush in the morning that saturates your body with peace. Despite everything that is happening right now, my head feels lighter and, to be perfectly cheesy, for a brief moment I feel happy to be alive.

The jagged cliffs have layers of brilliant red and orange with dots of green plants and trees. Travis is absolutely captivated. "This does kind of look like the Grand Canyon," he says.

We pass the stacked yellow flowers of the kāhili ginger and tall trunks of eucalyptus trees. Soon we are swallowed by the grove of giant ferns; it's like a scene in *Jurassic Park*. While we continue our hike, I tell Travis about Celia, how she was so awful to me and that Sammie told me that she was cheating on Luke. And about Wynn Hightower's multimillion-dollar project to decimate the natural beauty of the North Shore. Could the quiet title lawsuits have prompted a dissenter to kill Wynn's son for revenge?

Travis comes to a stop. "Listen, can we talk about something else? I mean, no offense, but this whole thing is kind of a downer."

"Ah, this downer is what my family is dealing with. What I'm dealing with."

"It's practically over, right? Your dad is innocent, and his lawyer will take care of his defense."

"It's not so easy, Travis. I mean, your mom's a therapist—"

"Well, technically a psychologist."

" 'K, psychologist, and your dad's a college professor and everyting makes sense. I mean, a straight line is just dat, straight. But for us Santiagos, it's not so simple."

"It's because you are making it complicated. Leilani, you are your own person. You need to create boundaries between yourself and your family."

"Uh, you're so frustrating." The path is now made up

of slippery smooth rocks in red dirt. Pools of water have accumulated in crevices between the stones, so both of us stay quiet as we make sure that we don't lose our footing.

We are behind Waipoʻo Falls, not in front of it. Small streams run toward the head of the waterfall. In front of us is a small waterfall pouring down black volcanic rock into a small pool. Birds sing overhead, and the smell of the yellow kāhili ginger flowers is intoxicating.

"Man, that's so beautiful."

It is. The beauty catches my throat. Taking off our hiking boots and socks, we dip our toes in the pool of freezing cold water. The exercise has left us thirsty and hungry, and I take out my full water bottle and the energy bars generously provided by our Airbnb Superhosts.

"I don't want to fight, Leilani," Travis says after taking a swig of water. "I'm only here for you. To support you."

We hike back to the car, and I drive Travis to the front view of the falls. Other tourists have gathered there, and Travis agrees to take a photo of a family from Texas. The water cascading down the red-orange cliffs is spectacular; there's absolutely no place on earth like Waimea Canyon. I've never been to the Grand Canyon, but I'm convinced that it can't be as beautiful as this.

"I'm getting hungry," Travis comments, and I look down at my phone. At least three people have texted me about the luau at Waimea Junction.

"Our landlord is having luau today. There's kalua pig and everything."

"Is that when they roast a pig in the ground?"

I nod.

"Hell, yeah, I'm in. I'll get to see where you work, too."

"It's nothing special. I mean, it's a shack." I don't know

why I'm dissing my family's business. It's lasted three generations, whereas most eateries don't last three years.

By the time we arrive, the roasted kalua pig is ready
for its unveiling in back of Waimea Junction. Pekelo, Kelly,
their friends, and my dad are shoveling dirt and hot rocks
off of the pig, which is wrapped in chicken wire and banana
leaves. It smells so good. "Dis gonna broke da mouth," I
murmur to myself.

"What did you say?" Travis asks me.

"Oh, that it's gonna be delicious."

"Ono kau kau," says a small person by my side. It's
Mama Liu, wearing a neon pink T-shirt, tan clam diggers,
and oversize sunglasses that competitive cyclists wear. Her
wardrobe is composed of clothing found in unclaimed luggage in her taxi.

"Oh, howzit, Mama Liu?" She's literally licking her lips
in anticipation of the food.

"Waimea Junction popular place these days," she says.

I have no idea what she is getting at.

She pulls me aside, and Travis is so transfixed by the
digging out of the kalua pig that he doesn't notice.

"I picked up big-shot money man from the airport and
dropped him off here."

I'm thinking that she's talking about Wynn Hightower.
"When?"

"The day before his boy got killed."

What? That didn't make sense. I knew that he had been
on Kaua'i for business, but why in the world would Wynn
Hightower come to Waimea Junction?

"Gave me an extra fifty to keep my mouth shut." She
grins, revealing her yellow and brown teeth.

Mr. Hightower, I think, *that was the worst fifty-dollar*

investment of your life.

"Do you know who he spoke to?"

Mama Liu shakes her head. "Got one oddah call, so I go."

Why did Wynn Hightower come to Waimea Junction on Friday? Before I leave the luau tonight, I'm sure as hell going to find out.

Chapter Eleven

"You wanna see da pig head?" Dani asks Travis, and I'm surprised that Travis is actually game. Dani takes him through the back door into Santiago's, where I think the head is probably cooling in the fridge for some of Grand-pop Santiago's relatives to make *sisig*, a traditional Filipino dish.

Uncle Rick appears from the side of the imu. His face is red, and I don't know if that's from the sun, heat, or maybe liquor. I nod to him.

"Foot okay?" he asks.

"Yah, like brand-new. Tanks for da oddah day."

"You see Auntie Barbara?"

"She here?" Dad really went all out to invite everyone. Since his activity is so limited by his ankle bracelet, he is making sure that people are coming to him.

Uncle Rick excuses himself to find her, and I kind of wonder what the big deal is. At a luau, people go from one corner to another. I need to find the corner where men and women are preparing the kalua pig for the crowd.

While Kelly is setting up the giant rice cookers in back of Killer Wave, Pekelo is at the table, using tongs to tear the soft meat off the cooked pig. He's wearing a tank top, revealing all his tattoos on his arms and back. I see King Kamehameha, Queen Lili'uokalani, and two more recent tats of his parents with halos over their heads. Mr. and Mrs.

Kahuakai tragically died within six months of each other last year—the husband of complications from diabetes, and the wife, a heart attack.

"I need to talk to you," I say to him. Since he was at Killer Wave last Friday, he might have seen Wynn Hightower.

"Supa busy right now," he says, his cigarette tipping out of his mouth. I want a cigarette, too, but I don't dare with both my dad and Travis close by.

"Later den. It's important." I'm not sure that he's listening to me, but I'll track him down.

"Eh, Pekelo, watch da ash," my dad scolds him from across the way.

Farther down the food prep line is Sean, surrounded by some twentysomething women, some former high school classmates of mine. They were the ones who studied hula, belonged to a hālau, wore their dark hair long down to their waists. They fit the stereotype of the ideal woman from Hawai'i, the one in grass skirts on travel brochures. Sean sees me and waves a plastic gloved hand my way. Of course he's smiling. He's in paradise.

I don't know why I feel jealous. I'm with Travis. Why should I care that Sean is surrounded by beautiful women?

"Leilani Santiago?" A woman wearing long pants and a button-down shirt comes over and stands next to me. She's up to no good in an outfit like that at a luau, and it turns out I'm right. She identifies herself as a reporter for one of the local newspapers. "I was at Wynn Hightower's press conference and I saw you getting arrested. I wanted to ask you a few questions."

I check if anyone might have heard her. I walk her down to the far end of the property. Is she pupule? How could she come to Waimea Junction—during a luau, no less—for an interview?

I cross my arms and face her. Like me, she wears hardly any makeup. Her hair is cut in a straight bob and her cheeks are dotted with acne scars. She wouldn't win any beauty contests, but then I wouldn't, either. "You shouldn't be here. This is a private event."

She glances back at the varied collection of random people, ancient surfers, baachans and jiichans, babies, even homeless people. Hell, I don't know half the people there. "Really?" she says.

"What do you want?"

"I had written up a story about the protest, but my editor killed it. He said that my job was to write about the new development and how it would be good for the local economy."

Why should I care that your news company is so shady, I think.

"I think there's something more to Wynn Hightower. I've been doing research on him, the way he does business. I think you have information on him, too. We can help each other."

"So your editor can reject another story?"

"No, I want to take it to another department. News instead of business."

"I have no information," I tell her. "Only that he's an asshole. And you can quote me on that."

The reporter's lips form a straight line. I'm not giving her what she wants. She hands me her company business card. "Taylor Ogura," it reads, "Business Reporter." "If you change your mind, get in touch. My cell phone's on there."

I watch her walk back to the luau and feel sorry for

her. If she's looking for any confidential news sources, she's come to the wrong place.

I return to Santiago's to get Travis, but both he and Dani have disappeared. Baachan has set up a card table inside of the shack for a game of *pepito*, kind of like Filipino poker. One of her ukulele-playing friends is at the game, and two young men—one of them is Andy Mabalot. How dare he set foot in our place after literally arresting both my dad and me? But that's how it is in Waimea. We've grown up with each other and sometimes that's enough, at least for a game of cards. Baachan, who seems to be winning, has resorted to her special strategy—placing her dentures in a glass of water to distract the other players.

I leave Santiago's and go into Lee's Leis and Flowers. Court must have done bouquets for a wedding this morning, because the scent of stephanotis, the white wedding flower, lingers in the shop. She sits alone at her worktable, stringing leftover flowers into a lei, which she often does at the end of the day. She's delighted to see me and invites me to sit with her to talk story and share her plate of poke—not the fake Mainland kind with avocado and other nonsense, but seasoned with chopped kukui nut and the tendrils of ogo, as fresh as the sea.

"Your dad seems okay," she says as I claim one of the folding chairs around the table. In addition to the random flower heads, the table holds rolls of green floral tape and a metal thorn and leaf stripper, which resembles a giant staple remover.

"Ho no. He has to wear one ankle bracelet. Only allowed to go from Santiago's and home."

"Eh, sorry, Leilani." A yellow cymbidium bloom joins a purple orchid on her string of flowers.

"Gotta find out who wen kill Luke Hightower. Den it'll all be ova," I say, more for my benefit than Court's. "You know Andy Mabalot next door playing pepito with Baachan dem?"

Next comes a couple of red carnations. "Oh, yah?" Court is not surprised.

I tell her that there are no leads in Luke's murder investigation. I'm frustrated as hell. "Maybe instead of taking money from Baachan, he should try for work some."

"He not losing to your baachan."

We both laugh. That was for sure. Once he starts winning, Baachan will make sure he'll be out of the game.

"Mama Liu is here, too," I announce.

"Oh, yah? Once she hears of free grindz—"

"She wen tell me she drove Wynn Hightower here last Friday. You wen see him?"

She purses her lips and puts the lei down to check her calendar on her phone. "I had a retirement party at the community center. Kelly wen help me dat day."

I now remember. Pekelo was filling in for Kelly at Killer Wave.

I watch as Court finishes and ties the two ends of her lei together.

"Howzit going with Travis?" she asks.

"Good. We staying at one pretty place up on da hill. Went hiking in the canyon." I lift my hiking boots, now coated in red dirt as proof.

With any other girlfriend, that would be an adequate answer. But Court must sense that there's more because she doesn't react.

"Out of Seattle, he different," I finally admit.

Still nothing. She's my only local friend who's visited

me in Washington, and I want to hear what's on her mind.

"You one different person in Seattle," she finally offers.

"Well, yeah. I'm not the same person I was in high school."

"I know dat. But in Seattle, it seems . . . like you shame you from Hawai'i."

"Dat's bulai." I can't believe my sweet Court is saying something so outrageous.

"Right dea. No way you would say 'bulai' on the Mainland."

"That's because no one understand. It's called code switching, Court." "Code switching," changing from one dialect or language, is actually something Travis taught me.

"I dunno about code switching bullshit," Court says, "but I know *you* switch and I not talking just your words. When you not hea, you no even tink about us. Wen you stay in Seattle, you no make a place for us."

"That's not true."

"When I wen visit, did you ask me where I like go?"

"We went to Pike's Market, Underground Tour, Mariner's game."

"I wanted for go to Space Needle and Nordstroms."

"But dat's tourist trap. So expensive for go Space Needle. Not worth it."

"Dat's what Travis said, and you went along wid him. You nevah back me up."

I think about what Court is saying. I'm replaying our time in Seattle together in my mind. I hate to admit it, but I think she's right.

"Why you nevah say anyting?"

"Because he's your man. I no like talk stink about him." She stands up and starts putting her floral tools away. "Mo' important, what's happening with you and Sean?"

"Whatchu tryin' for say?"

"I see, Leilani. I know you. Are you sure maybe Sean da problem between you and Travis?"

We hear a commotion next door at Santiago's. We both rush outside. It's Dad helping Uncle Rick from the floor of the shave shack, with Auntie Barbara a few steps behind. A broken beer bottle is on the floor, and Court grabs a spare bucket to place the shards of glass out of people's way. Sophie and Ro squat next me. I appreciate their help but tell them to watch themselves. "Sophie, get me a wet rag," I say, and she goes to the sink and runs water over a dish towel.

She squats down and hands me the towel. "Auntie Barbara sure likes to drink," she whispers in my ear.

No, that's Uncle Rick, I feel like telling Sophie, but I don't respond.

She senses my disbelief. "I smelled alcohol on her breath when we went ova dea," she whispers again.

I frown. My little sister must be confused. In light of everything that has happened, I don't blame her.

After we clean up the broken grass, I apologize to Court for not listening to her on her Seattle trip.

"No worries. You still da best."

After we hug it out, I weave through the crowd to find Travis.

Mom is sitting at the picnic table with D-man. She's sipping some kind of orange-green drink, probably full of kale that D-man whipped up special for her. Before Mom was diagnosed, I don't think D-man even knew what kale was.

Dad is approaching the picnic table, carrying two plates full of shredded kalua pig, scoops of white rice, poi, and lomi-lomi salmon. The table, however, is full. I'm not sure that there's a place for him.

I finally find Travis at D-man's, drinking with a bunch of old surfers. One of D-man's employees, Malcolm, is manning the bar.

"Leilani, come here," the men call me over.

OhmyGod, really?

Travis moves halfway on his stool to give me room. I'm not going to sit butt to butt with him in front of this crowd. "C'mon, Leilani, have some fun," he urges. He orders some tequila, my downfall, for both of us. "I see you running around, taking care of people. You don't have to do that, you know."

I stare at my shot glass of tequila. "That's easy for you to say."

He looks at me incredulously. "Oh, not again. I'm privileged, blah, blah, blah."

"You're drunk." I hate it when he gets like this.

D-man has returned to relieve Malcolm, and he's able to quickly assess what's going on. "Hey, brah, maybe go easy on the tequila."

Travis stares at him and downs his shot. He turns his empty glass over and orders another one. D-man is not going to budge.

Somehow seeing Travis through D-man's eyes makes me feel ashamed. All those late nights at bars when Travis drank one too many. I made excuses for him. He was stressed out at work. It was a long weekend and time for him to cut loose. But really I was scared to lose him if I made a fuss. I was so blind, but now the scales are falling from my eyes.

"Just because you got arrested and went to jail, you

think that you're down with the people."

"I'm going," I say and walk out to the back by the dumpster and recycle shed for Waimea Junction. Something familiar is stuck in the corner, and I do a double take. Held in place by the top of the blue recycle bin is our missing shave ice mold, the possible murder weapon that killed Luke Hightower.

I run through the back door of Santiago's and demand that Andy come with me to the recycling shed.

"Eh, I winnin', Leilani." I glance at his hand and it's good, but I don't care.

"I think I've found da murder weapon in da recycle shed. Maybe it's got fingerprints."

"Outside? Wen rain hard da oddah day. Da evidence probably gone."

"Inside da shed. And da shed's all metal."

"Go check'um, go." Baachan is only too willing to have Andy leave the game during his winning streak. Her dentures are still floating in their glass next to her stack of quarters.

Andy must have felt some relief that I was talking to him again, because he grudgingly agrees to come with me. We walk through kids running around barefoot and pass the red-faced surfers hanging out at D-man's.

Trash bags probably filled with beer and liquor bottles from the luau are left in front of the metal shed. Broken-down cardboard boxes line the left side of the shed, and the shave ice mold is still there, sitting on top of the recycle tub like a crooked crown.

"Look like one regular plastic container."

"It's not. I know. I deal with dem every single damn day."

Andy sighs and gets on his cell phone to report it. "Yah, yah," I hear him say. "I see you at da station."

He gets one of the collapsed boxes and folds it back into shape. With some plastic gloves from the cooking crew, he delicately places the mold into the box. "We see, Leilani. Dis a big long shot."

Carrying the box, Andy heads for his car, which is parked alongside the highway, and I follow. "You no can come."

I hold my ground. "I stay going already."

Andy shrugs his shoulders and we continue on to his yellow jeep.

"Sergeant Toma's not gonna like dis," he says as I snap on the seat belt.

"He doesn't like anyting I do, so notting new."

Andy can't argue with that and starts the jeep.

I stay quiet for a few minutes while he drives. "You knew ice was da murder weapon."

Andy nods. "From cold water melting underneath Luke's body. Cause of death was epidural hematoma. Rememba Eric Chong from high school got hit wid da baseball and wen die a few days later?"

I remember. It was such a freak accident.

"Whoever wen hit Luke, got into his brain. He probably died a few hours after da initial trauma."

"What time?"

"I no can tell you everyting, Leilani." We pass by signs saying "Kalaheo."

"I sent Sammie Nunes to you." I feel like I should get credit for that.

"Yah, tanks, what she wen share makes sense wid their text messages, fo' sure."

"Somebody must have been following Luke." I get chicken skin from thinking that someone could have been stalking him outside our house.

"Yah, so keep your eyes open."

The jeep lurches over a pothole in the road, and I turn to check on the mold on the backseat. Still safe in the box.

"You know your whole family's fingerprints probably on dat mold."

"But there might be someone else's. Someone who had no business touchin' our shave ice molds.

"What about Luke's cell phone?" I add. "You must have found someting on dat."

"Notting that incriminates your dad."

"So you think my faddah's innocent."

"I dunno. He may be, Leilani. Dat's da best I can do."

I'll take that for now.

I go inside the police station with Andy, but have to stay in the lobby. Even though I'm furious at him, I text Travis to tell him where I am. I'm not surprised when I don't get a reply. When he starts to drink like this, it's hard for him to stop.

Andy, his hand in his back pocket, emerges.

"What he wen say?"

"He already went home, but I entered da evidence."

We get back into the jeep. This was uneventful. Andy was right: I didn't have to come with him.

On the ride back, Andy gets more talkative. "I feel bad,

Leilani. I didn't want to do dat to you in Po'ipū. But you gotta understand, Mr. Hightower has plenty power, sway."

"I nevah heard of him before all dis."

"Because lotta of those big shots hide behind other names."

Like Bamboo Royal Hills.

Andy decides that he doesn't want to return to the pe-pito game, and I want to call it a night, too. But I do need to find Travis. Andy drops me off and I surprise myself by thanking him. "Mahalo, 'night."

One of our family friends has set up a portable kara-oke machine outside by D-man's bar. Only the diehards, extremely drunk, still remain. No sign of Travis. Waimea Junction is totally trashed. It's going to take all day tomor-row to gather all the dirty paper plates, crushed Solo cups, and empty beer bottles.

My car is still there; it's about the only one parked along the highway. As I drive back to the Airbnb, I rehearse what I'm going to say to Travis. *You can't treat me that way in public. You're being disrespectful. When you drink too much, you become ugly.*

Sean's van is in his driveway, and I can't help but won-der if one of those sexy wahine from the luau is in his house. *Not my business*, I remind myself.

I find Travis on the bed, still in his skinny jeans and T-shirt. Based on how much he's snoring, he's stone drunk.

For my own quality of sleep, I go into another bed-room, one facing west. I still toss and turn, and even though I'm away from Travis's snoring, I'm still with him in my thoughts. I usually make big decisions based on my gut feelings, and my gut is telling me things I don't necessarily want to hear.

I'm not sure if I've slept at all when my phone dings. Without knowing what time it is, I pick it up. It's a text from Nori, of all people:

Hear about PAPA Sorry

What the hell? He must be high, I think. Then another ding. He's sent me a photo. *Probably something obscene.* But I tap on the image to make it bigger.

Is that who I think it is? I sit up and turn on the lamp. I let out an f-bomb. It is, indeed, Wynn Hightower, naked, and in a very compromising position with his son's girlfriend, Celia Johnson, also naked.

I have no idea where Nori is, but I immediately call him.

"Nori, this is Leilani Santiago."

"Who?"

"Wan-Wan-chan."

He begins to laugh. Jerk. He probably knew it was me but wanted to hear me say his nickname for me out loud.

"Why did you text this photo of Luke's father with Celia? And when did you take it?"

"I send to Luke on Saturday."

"You mean the Saturday he was killed?"

"*Hai.*"

"So you knew that they were having an affair."

"I told Luke a week ago something strange going on. He didn't believe. Got mad at me and everyone else. I was at Bamboo Royal when I hear something funny in Celia's room. I do not remember taking this photo. Don't even remember sending to Luke. Check my phone today, and there it is!"

"Don't erase it, Nori. Keep it on your phone, okay?"

"Okay, okay. Luke was my best friend." Nori's voice takes on a somber tone, and I think he's high again.

"Where are you, by the way?"

"Cali-for-nia."

"Do you think Mr. Hightower might have killed his son? Or maybe Celia?"

"All I hear is your father arrested. Not fair." He keeps jumping around, and it's hard to follow what he's saying.

"Thank you, Nori. And keep in touch, okay?"

"Bye bye, *Wan-Wan-chan*."

Turns out it's nine o'clock and I have no idea if Sean is a morning person or not, but he's going to get an early visitor. He is a morning person, because he answers the door on my first knock. He's dressed in a fresh T-shirt that has the words "Giant Robot" in script across his chest. The curls on his head are wet.

"Well, hello."

"Mornin'," I say.

"You disappeared last night. I heard you might have found something that could help in the investigation."

"I received a text that may help, too."

He freely invites me in, and I breathe a little sigh of relief that he seems to be by himself.

He has made some green tea, and even though I'm not a tea person, I accept the Japanese-style cup he serves it in. Instead of the tea bag Baachan uses, he brews it with loose tea leaves. I'm careful to place the hot cup on a coaster on the koa wood table.

"Nori texted this to Luke on Saturday." I slide my phone over to him.

Sean pushes his glasses up to get a good look with his naked eye. He turns the phone slightly to fully absorb what's going on, and I finally pull it out of his hand.

"That's why Luke gave the surfboard to my dad. He was pissed off and wanted to be free of anything related to his own father."

"And then what? His father comes to Waimea Junction and they have a fight?"

"Not sure. If only I knew what was on his cell phone—"

"Well, the police know. Forward this photo to them."

"I don't know. Wynn Hightower has a lot of influence, even within the police department."

"If they don't look into it, we'll hold them accountable."

I don't know which warms my heart more—"hold them accountable" or "we."

I take a sip of the tea. It's super bitter, but I think I can get used to it.

After drinking his tea, Sean has something to share with me. "Hey, so I spoke to that dealer last night. The one who has the surfboard. He wouldn't tell me who's interested in it, but I think I'm going to pay him a visit. He may be convinced to share more info if I show him some green."

My face must have looked as clueless as I felt.

"Leilani, money."

"Oh yah, of course." Another sip of the tea. Now I think that I can't get used to it.

"I also gave a couple of names of lawyers to your father."

"You did?"

"Yeah, last night. One's actually on Kaua'i."

I reach out for his hand and gently squeeze. "Mahalo. I appreciate it." I realize that I may have been too affection-ate and pull my hand back.

"Your boyfriend seemed like he was having a good time," Sean says.

I cringe. "What did he do?"

"Someone brought out a karaoke machine and he was really into it."

Sounds about right.

"He also kind of spilled the beans about you being arrested."

Shit. "You mean while he had the mic? Did my parents hear?"

"I'm pretty sure they did."

That's the last thing I need to deal with.

I get up. "I betta go and send this photo to Andy Mabalot." I notice that the sales folder from the Hightower Enterprises press conference in Poʻipū is on his kitchen counter. "Hey, can I borrow this?"

"Sure. Go ahead."

I quickly leaf through the contents, trying to find an address for Hightower's real estate company.

"What are you looking for?"

"Do you know where Hightower's office is located?"

"He has one at the Poʻipū hotel, but I think he mostly does business at his house in Hanalei."

Of course there's no address for his personal residence in the press releases.

"I have his home address. You want it? I can text it to you."

It occurs to both of us that we haven't exchanged phone numbers. I almost blush as I give him my digits. *C'mon, Leilani, get a grip*, I tell myself. *You're not in high school anymore.*

When I return to the Airbnb, Travis is in the living room, lying on the hibiscus-patterned couch with a plastic bag filled with ice cubes on his forehead.

"Where were you?" he asks.

"I've been doing some thinking."

"That doesn't sound good."

"Are you okay? Here, I'll make you some coffee," I tell him.

This time we don't sit outside on the deck, but around a breakfast nook in the bright white kitchen.

Instead of drinking the coffee, I wrap my fingers around the mug to feel its warmth. Travis, on the other hand, still holds the bag of ice on his forehead while taking slow, loud sips of his coffee. I'm not sure that I can do this. I proceed the only way I know how: headfirst. "When we were together in Seattle, I felt that we were totally together. Of the same mind."

"We were. We are."

"No, I don't think so now. I think I might have lost myself in Seattle."

Travis lowers the bag of ice from his eyes. "You're back home and you're confused."

"I am confused, that's true. But I may have been confused in Seattle, too. I'm trying to find where I belong."

"You don't want to stay here. I mean, it's beautiful to visit, Leilani, but for your future. . . ."

"The thing is, Travis, I'm not sure about my future. I mean, back in Seattle, I'm just in admin. I can do admin anywhere."

"You can finish up at UW. Get your bachelor's and go for something you really want."

"I have no idea what that is. I don't know what's going to happen to my family, our house, but I think I need to be on Kaua'i, Waimea."

"Listen, I can tell you this much—your future's not in shaved ice."

I summon all my strength not to correct him to say "shave." "How do you know?"

Travis raises his eyebrows. "So, what, are we breaking up?"

"I think so."

Chapter Twelve

"I didn't think it would end like this. That I would come to Kaua'i for us to break up," Travis says as I follow the signs to the Lihue Airport. He was able to change his flight to a day earlier. He doesn't want to stay one more night in paradise.

"Are you sure? Wasn't there a little part of you, maybe a tiny percent, that was thinking that we would?" I guide the Ford to the front of the terminal.

"I don't know. Maybe a little part. Maybe I thought that if I didn't come, we would break up for sure."

My stomach feels upset. I'm not sure if it's from the decision to end our relationship or Sean's bitter green tea. Or maybe both.

"Don't get out of the car. Just drop me off." He directs me to the curb for passenger loading and unloading.

That's fine with me. I don't want to have a breakdown in public outside of the TSA checkpoint.

He gets out and goes to retrieve his duffel bag from the backseat. I hurry to open the window to tell him goodbye, but he has already slammed the car doors, turned away, and started walking toward the terminal. Families hug, kiss, and wave their goodbyes to one another. Even a hotel van driver sends tourists home with a shaka. I wait at the curb until airport security tells me that I have to leave.

The tears do come, harder than I expect. I can barely see the road through my tears and finally stop at Pakala Beach. I park on the side of the highway and go down a trail through some tall grasses and banyan trees to the water. Mostly locals go to the Infinities break here, and only when the surf is good, which it isn't right now. I plop down in the sand and stare at the small breaking waves.

Have I made a mistake? Have I thrown almost two years of my adult life away by breaking it off with Travis? For a second, I feel like calling him and telling him that we should rethink this whole thing.

I remember what Court said. That I'm different in Seattle. I'm tired of being different in two places. Somehow these two, or maybe more, parts of me need to finally come together.

I can think of only one person in my life who may possibly understand. I get my phone out and press my sister's name, but I get her voicemail. A few seconds later, Emily calls me back.

"Did you call me? You didn't leave a message."

Just hearing her voice makes me start to cry again.

"Leilani, what's wrong? Is it Dad?"

No, no, I tell her. And slowly, bits and pieces of my long-distance relationship with Travis roll out, the bumps, turns, and terrible potholes. And now the severed relationship, me taking a sharp knife and cutting it before it can grow further.

"Are you sure that it's really ended? Maybe you'll get back together when you get some space."

I shake my head. Travis and I only seem to make sense

when we are together in Seattle. Our rhythms of life and our habits move in established grooves there. When one of us is away, our relationship gets off the tracks and starts spinning out of control. Perhaps our love is only for a certain place and time. Maybe I really decided to move back home to make a clean break from him.

"Court says I'm different when I'm on the Mainland." Damn, and I think she's right. "It's like I erase a big part of myself there, some parts that I needed to hold on to."

"I know how you feel. Maybe I don't feel like a different person in California, but maybe a different version. It's helped that I hang out with other students from Hawai'i sometimes. The best part is that we don't have to explain things to each other."

We share a moment of silence and understanding. I'm already starting to feel better.

"Do you regret going back home?" Emily asks me.

I have to think about it. I do miss the dark secrets of Seattle, the discovery of a new pop-up restaurant, the music scene, the independent bookstores. But being reunited with the sun and surf of Kaua'i has been healing, too. Also, there's been Sean Cohen. I tell Emily more about him.

"So, what, are you into him?"

"No, well, I'm not sure. Gotta say it's nice to have a new friend. A friend that doesn't know me from elementary school or high school."

"Someone who you can start with from scratch," Emily affirms.

My phone dings with a message. It's a new caller, with a 408 area code. Sean with Wynn Hightower's address.

"K den, have to go, Emily. There's some business I have to take care of."

Wynn Hightower's exact address, given to me by Sean, doesn't show up on my GPS. *Does he have enough power to control satellite signals?* I wonder. At least I can make it over to his general neighborhood in Hanalei Bay.

Bamboo Royal was one thing—a Japanese-style pagoda amid old sugarcane fields growing wild—but this exclusive area is something else entirely. Every blade of grass, every flower, looks well tended, pruned, and fertilized. Nothing living has escaped the eyes of the masters of the land. And that includes humans as well.

I'm wandering on the street, checking over the street addresses. Even the birds must be outfitted with security cameras, because I'm obviously spotted and watched. Wynn emerges from a walkway surrounded by tall hedges.

"I suppose you're looking for me," he says. He wears a short-sleeved shirt and khaki shorts. "Well, don't keep standing out there like a stalker. If you want to talk to me, come inside." He turns back to his walkway, and I figure that I need to follow.

Within the confines of his property is an expansive yard, the lawn the greenest green I've ever seen. Fruit trees heavy with mangoes, bananas, and lychee line one side, while on the other are bushes of creamy plumeria, bright red hibiscus, and lobster-claw flowers. If this weren't Wynn Hightower's property, I'd think it was the Garden of Eden.

The house is one story but looks wide and expansive. There's a large covered porch that surrounds the property. Through the door is an open interior layout with ceiling fans in every zone.

Wynn practically herds me through a side door into a

room that is obviously his home office. There's a whiteboard with dates and names associated with his various development projects—not only in Hawai'i, but also California—that dominates one wall. He has a large desk, the kind that I only see on television shows, arrayed with various golf, surfing, and real estate trophies and awards. He points to one of two padded chairs and almost commands me to sit while he takes his position behind the desk.

"What the hell are you doing here?" he asks.

I take out my phone and show him the photo that Nori has texted. "Do you know that Luke received this the day he was killed? He knew about you and Celia."

He tries to grab the phone from my hand.

"Don't even bother. I've already sent it to the police," I tell him.

He plops down again into his top-of-the-line ergonomic chair. "Having an extramarital relationship is not a crime," he says. "And the police know all about it."

My heart falls. I was counting on this being key evidence that turns the murder investigation around. If the police are already aware of their relationship, what's keeping them from considering Wynn a person of interest?

"I don't get you," I murmur. "Why are you still here, doing business as usual?"

"Ms. Santiago, don't purport to know anything about me. Kaua'i is my second home. My great-grandfather worked here. He was a doctor here. He saved and improved the lives of plantation workers. Even though he was from the Mainland, Kaua'i was where he always wanted to be. His love for this place has been passed down the generations to my family. So even though our home base is in Orange County, my goal was always to return to Kaua'i.

"I know you judge me based on the color of my skin, but many of these other descendants, those claiming to have kuleana ties, have never stepped foot on these lands before."

Maybe they never had a chance to, I think. *Perhaps they didn't have the family wealth to return and buy hotels.*

"I could never do business after someone from my family died so recently," I say.

His face completely changes. All the hard lines soften, and his jaw and chin almost seem to dissolve in the wrinkles of his neck. He seems really old now, less George Clooney like. "Don't tell me how to grieve my only son's death. You have no right."

I consider what he has just said to me. As much as I hate to admit it, I probably have stepped over the line. All of the confidence that I had earlier has disappeared. Without saying goodbye, I leave his office and home. As I continue down the walkway, there is Mrs. Hightower, wearing a floppy cotton hat and capri pants, kneeling down to trim some low-growing flowers.

I try to be as inconspicuous as possible, but how can she ignore someone walking from her front door?

"You're Tommy's daughter, aren't you?" she says.

I nod my head. I remember that my dad had promised Luke's mother that he would take care of him.

"How is he doing?"

I'm frozen and I can barely speak. "Okay," I say.

"Give him my regards." She returns to her clipping, and tearing out a random weed here and there. *This is beyond bizarre*, I think as I get into the car. The mother of a surfer whom my father is charged with killing offers her regards. It dawns on me. She knows. She knows that my father is falsely accused. Why is she keeping silent?

When I'm back in the car, I find the business card in my wallet and make a phone call. "Hello, Taylor, it's Lei-lani Santiago. I have some information that I would like to share with you."

I meet Taylor in a local plate-lunch place in an industrial area in Līhu'e. She tells me that she's starving and hasn't eaten anything all day. "You want something?" she asks, but not like she means it.

"Maybe a bottle of water." I stake out a quiet spot among the picnic tables outside. My stomach is still queasy, and although the food looks and smells great, I figure that I'd better take it easy.

After about fifteen minutes, Taylor comes out of the place with a Styrofoam container, its compartments over-flowing with loco moco, beef stew, and macaroni salad. The girl obviously likes to eat. "What?" she says after seeing the expression on my face. "I told you I was hungry."

I take sips of water and watch her devour her late lunch. She's light on personal grooming. It's like she slept funny on her hair but didn't bother to put a brush through it when she woke up. Again, no makeup except for some lip gloss—or maybe that's just the grease from the loco moco gravy. I recognize the clothes that she's wearing, or at least they're the same type as from the luau. I'm getting the feeling that Taylor Ogura is really not a bundle of fun.

She finally slows down to catch her breath and take a swig of her passion fruit drink. "So, what you got?"

I enlarge the photo of Wynn and Celia and slide my

phone over to her.

She takes one look and makes a face. "This is all you have for me?"

"What do you mean? It's a compromising photo of Mr. Hightower with his son's girlfriend."

"Everyone knows that Wynn is a player. That's not news. We're not a tabloid; we've been around for more than a hundred years."

I don't mean to, but I halfway roll my eyes.

"Listen, a rich white married guy sleeping with a girl who is young enough to be his daughter. Do you think anyone gives a shit?"

Taylor must think I'm ultra-naive and unsophisticated. A shave ice girl and that's it.

She finishes chewing her food. "I thought that you had something on the quiet title properties. You know, something related to Bamboo Royal Hills. Hightower's working with a professor at Kaua'i Community College to find all the descendants to offer them a deal. The professor actually has kuleana ties to the land himself. Wants to help clear up all the challenges to the property."

"No kiddin'." How strange to think that a native Hawaiian academic would want to help Hightower build his real estate monstrosity in such a pristine and peaceful part of Kaua'i.

"I actually saw Wynn today," I say.

"You what?" Taylor drops her plastic fork in her last bit of beef stew.

"I went to Wynn's home office. Hanalei Bay."

"You had an appointment?"

"No, I just went there."

"You have balls, I'll give you that much. What'd he say?"

"That the police know about his affair."

Taylor gives me a look, *I told you so.*

"And that his family has long ties to Kaua'i."

"Oh, don't tell me, his great-grandfather was a doctor who saved all these native Hawaiian lives?"

I nod.

"I've looked into that. Many plantation workers didn't get the medical care they needed. I love how Wynn Hightower likes to twist that story."

I fell for it. I may indeed be the country bumpkin Taylor thinks I am.

"Mrs. Hightower was at the house, too."

"Wow, you got the whole welcome party." She drains the last bit of her canned drink. "How closely did you look at the Bamboo Royal Hill's development plan?"

Ah—I saw the pretty computer-drawn images. I hate to admit that I really didn't read the rest of it that carefully.

"Didn't you see the residential facility in the back, Plumeria Falls?"

The name sounds familiar. I figured that it's a clubhouse of some kind.

"It's a home for autistic adults. The Hightowers have a daughter a couple of years older than Luke who's special needs. She lives in some facility in Orange County."

"You mean their idea is to move the daughter to Kaua'i?"

"I guess they want to spend their later years here with her nearby."

It's strange to think of the Hightowers as real people with problems. Up until Luke's death, they seemed so golden and blessed. Maybe they struggle with personal issues like the rest of us.

By this time, Taylor has finished her meal. Not a single macaroni is left in her Styrofoam container. "By the way, text me that photo."

"I thought it wasn't worth shit."

"Well, you never know."

I forward Nori's text to her. "Done," I say, and she checks her phone as it dings. We get up and she throws away her trash on our way to the parking lot.

"By the way, where are you from?" I ask.

"I don't think that's any of your business."

"Sorry, didn't know it was top secret." It amuses me that Taylor would be so annoyed by such a basic question when her job is to ask strangers such intrusive ones.

She gives in. "New Jersey. Why?"

I could tell that she's not from around here. I want to tell her, *Good for you. Be yourself in the Islands. Don't lose who you are.* But instead I say, "No reason," and head for the Ford. I stop and turn around. "Maybe we should hang out sometime," I call out to her.

She frowns, looking even more manly. She doesn't say anything, probably thinking that my invitation isn't worth a response.

It's been an exhausting day, and as I pull into our driveway, I relish escaping in my cave of a bedroom. While I take off my Crocs at the door, I hear my dad in the living room, "Leilani, come here. We need to talk to you."

When I hear that, I know it's something serious.

Sunken in our old, collapsing love seat are both my parents. I sit cross-legged on the jute rug and brace myself for what's to come.

Even though Dad is the one who calls me over, Mom does most of the talking. "We are worried about that boy, Travis. And about you, too," she says.

"We broke up. No *shinpai*," I say, using Baachan's Japanese phrase, "no worries."

"Travis likes to drink a lot."

"Well, what's there to do in Seattle? You know it rains all the time. He just got carried away at the luau. And like I said, we broke up."

Am I imagining that both Mom and Dad are breathing a sigh of relief?

"I need to take 'sponsibility," Dad says. "Since I drank, you lookin' for a guy like me."

OhmyGod. I cannot friggin believe this. Dad is saying the same kind of psychobabble that Travis has said to me in the past. "Good one, Dad. Which step is that in AA?"

"Leilani!" my mother scolds.

I feel so, so tired. The reality of the past few days falls down on me like loose bricks. Maybe I'm not my real person even in front of my family.

"You didn't tell us that you were arrested," Mom continues.

"I didn't want to worry you."

"You have no business with Wynn Hightower," Dad says. "Stay away from him."

That's a little late now. "Do you know how much stress I'm under?" I tell my parents. "Tryin' to keep Santiago's afloat, take care of the girls and Baachan? And you get arrested and the house is mortgaged. We're about to lose everyting."

I'm on a roll and I'm not going to stop. "And you, you

knew about Mr. Hightower and his cheatin' ways. Why didn't you tell me about him and Celia?"

"I dunno about Celia."

"But you knew that he was a cheater. I bet you say nevah say notting to da police."

"I nevah say anyting dat's not my business."

"Dis is your business! You like be in jail, away from Mom, Baachan, Sophie, and Dani?" I'm so mad that I leave myself out.

"Your father trying his best." Mom has now become Dad's biggest defender.

"What's your best? Hiding what happened at Uncle Rick's house on Saturday night? Something's not right. You're protecting someone."

Dad is stone-faced. He doesn't dare look me in the eyes. Now I know that I've come dangerously close to the truth.

"So be dat way!" I get up from the floor and go straight into my bedroom, slamming the door shut.

Small-kid move, Santiago, I tell myself. I'm embarrassed to be me right now.

That night I wake up with a mean stomachache, one that feels like long sharp needles are piercing my belly. All I ate tonight was some leftover okazu that Baachan had left in the fridge. I run to the bathroom and lift the toilet seat. I try to hurl but nothing comes out. *What the hell is wrong with me?* The ground below me seems to be shifting. I can't hold on to what I've known or who I've been.

Chapter Thirteen

I get a text around 7 a.m. Damn Sean Cohen and his early-morning ways. My head is pounding from not getting enough sleep. I should have straightened Sean out from the beginning and told him not to contact me before 10 a.m.

I glance at the text:

Story in the local paper about Wynn Hightower

There's an internet link.

I leave my phone on a crate, my makeshift bedside table, and turn over to sleep. The story will still be there in two, three hours.

I rest for another couple of hours, but I'm not sure if I really went to sleep. I pick up my phone and click on the link. Sure enough, it's Taylor Ogura's story. As she had said yesterday, she doesn't mention a thing about Wynn Hightower's illicit affair. Nori's photo of him and Celia together doesn't get any play on the web page, and I'm actually relieved about that.

The story is all about the quiet title lawsuits and how they affect kuleana landowners. I was curious about why they called it "quiet title," and in her reporting, Taylor explains it—a lawsuit can serve to "quiet" a native Hawaiian's claim to ancestral land. If they don't pony up the money to challenge the lawsuit, in essence they are forfeiting the land. Since these developers have a lot more available money, it makes sense that they either usually win or are able to offer some money to clear title.

According to Taylor's story, Wynn Hightower has filed fifty quiet title lawsuits—fifty! It makes me sad to think that land will be lost. After all, no one owned land at one time in Hawai'i. It was open to all. Now outsiders with the big bucks were coming in, and we have become the outsiders.

One woman, originally from Los Angeles, Alice Lindquist, is quoted as having a claim over an acre of land. "Lindquist is actually physically occupying the land with her girlfriend to make sure that it isn't bulldozed over to make way for Hightower's project," Taylor has written. "She, in fact, was arrested in the protest of Hightower's hotel in Po'ipū." Alice Lindquist must have been my neighboring jail mate.

With so much at stake, maybe someone did kill Luke to make a point. It was no secret that Luke was coming to the surf competition and that he was being coached by my father. Could someone have been lying in wait for him that night?

I make a phone call and Sean picks up immediately. "Hello," I say. "Listen, I'm not a mornin' person. I thought I'd set you straight on that."

"Oh, sorry, was it too early for me to text?"

His voice is so soft and apologetic, I feel bad that I came off so bitchy.

I hold the phone to my ear as I walk out of my room. The house is dead quiet, aside from baka Jimin crowing in the backyard. There's a note from my mom on the table: "Took the car to run some errands. Dad and Baachan are at work."

"No, thanks for the article. It was super interesting, actually. Wondered if you could spare some time to do investigative work with me."

"What kind of investigative work?"

"The kind around Bamboo Royal."

"What time do you want me to pick you up?"

Once I'm in the van's passenger seat, Sean offers me some green tea in a tumbler. Thankfully I've brought some coffee in my UW one so I can decline without telling him that his tea is more lethal than bug killer.

"Travis left already?" he asks once we are on the highway.

"Yeah," I say. "He had things to do." It doesn't seem right to tell Sean about our breakup. Like I'm opening a door to a room that hasn't been cleaned yet.

Neither one of us says much as we travel up to the North Shore. I still feel raw from my argument with my parents. *What do you want, Leilani?* That's a question that I still can't answer. All I know is that things can't continue the way they have been.

I roll down the window and feel the salt air run through my hair. Only nature can heal me right now. "Why did you decide to buy land in Waimea?" I ask Sean. "You probably could have bought something on the North Shore or Poʻipu."

"Yeah, I looked at Hanalei Bay and other parts of the North Shore, but I think I prefer Waimea. It's drier. Less touristy. And, of course, there's the Canyon."

The Canyon. The artery of the island, in my book.

"You've lived in Waimea your whole life?"

"I actually was in Seattle for five years. I went to UW

for a couple of years but never finished."

"I was wondering about all the Husky garb."

"Yah, I'm a bit of a nerd." Getting into UW is actually my biggest accomplishment; not graduating is my biggest failure. "How about you? Where did you go to college?"

"A place called Caltech."

"That's where the *Big Bang Theory* guys work! Pasadena, right?"

Sean looks a bit sheepish, and I realize that I've gone fangirl over a network TV show. So uncool. "Sorry, I know that's all pretend. So after that, you moved back to Sunnyvale?"

"My friend and I launched a start-up in my parents' garage. It kind of exploded after that."

It must have for Sean to practically retire in his twenties.

"So it's okay for your parents for you to move so far from them?"

"My sister's nearby. And she has twins. They have their hands full. I was actually close to my grandfather. He died earlier this year. He was the original Nazi hunter."

I roll up the window so I can clearly hear what Sean says next.

"He was in a Polish death camp during World War II. It was a miracle that he survived."

"Oh my God. That's so heavy, Sean." No wonder he's obsessed with what happened so many decades ago.

"He was only a kid, the only survivor in his whole family. Other people helped him out, and he was able to move to the United States. He eventually became a reference librarian."

"That's why you're into books!"

"He started using his research skills to help these Jewish groups find Nazis who had escaped to other countries
like the US. I figure the one last thing I can do in his honor
is find this guy who is hiding out in Hawai'i."

My respect for Sean expands. Maybe he will make
good on his promise not to tear down Waimea Junction and
make it into a resort or some other redevelopment project.

In less than an hour, Sean's navigation app has brought
us to Bamboo Royal. We get out of the van. There are only
a few cars parked in the lot, and I wonder if Celia and Rex
are still here.

"Wow, it's so gorgeous," Sean says as he takes some
photos with his phone.

I lift up my head and listen as the wind kicks up. "It's
like the ole sugarcane fields are talkin' to us, eh?" I turn
and see that Sean has aimed his camera phone toward me.
"What are you doin'? Don't take a photo of me!"

He switches his focus to the Japanese pagoda.

"You've never been inside Bamboo Royal?"

Sean shakes his head. "Been meaning to. It's been written up in so many travel blogs."

I glance at the small opening in the fallow sugar fields.
"I hate to say this because you've driven me all the way here,
but can I meet these folks on my own? I think they'll be
more open—"

"No, I get it. I'll be walking around, taking pictures."

I'm glad that I haven't offended him and make my way
through the fields into the clearing that Sophie had discovered. As soon as I step into it, the giant Patsy emerges, this
time with a huge conch shell.

"I don't have time to mess around, Miss Patsy. I gotta
talk to your girlfriend. It's important."

Patsy checks me out from head to toe. "Oh, you're the girl who was arrested with us."

"You also ran me and my little sister off this land before that."

"I didn't recognize you without the little one. You know, she may have a future in entertainment. Great bone structure."

That's the last thing that Sophie needs to hear. She already thinks she'll meet and marry Jimin—the performer, not the rooster—some day.

"Follow me."

I walk behind Patsy through a narrow path, the sugar-cane leaves whipping at my cheeks. I start having second thoughts. Maybe I should have had Sean accompany me.

Finally, we reach a bare hill that is mostly dirt. Three pop-up tents are lined up next to one another with two larger sleeping tents pitched on another side. Underneath the pop-ups is a long table with a portable propane gas stove. Bottles of beer and a carton of soy milk float amid a giant melting ice block in a metal tub. A cord, tied from one end of the tent to another, supports a line of laundry, mostly T-shirts and shorts, but also a couple of panties. Based on their size, they are probably Patsy's.

"Alice, we have a visitor."

The middle-aged redheaded woman I spoke to in jail steps out of one of the tents. She's wearing a pink tank top and matching shorts. I now see a strip of white along the roots of her part. I guess it's hard to maintain your dye job in the middle of nowhere. "Oh, you," she says.

"Leilani Santiago," I extend my hand. "We spoke in jail."

"I remember. Alice Lindquist." We shake hands and

Alice offers me a seat on a fabric collapsible camping chair. She gets comfortable in a matching one.

Once I sit down, Patsy slips an ice-cold beer into my chair's cup holder.

"Maybe a little too early for that," I say but agree to a glass of fresh-squeezed orange juice instead. "How long have you been living this way?"

"Three months, but it seems forever." Alice says "forever" in a good way. "The rat race of Los Angeles was killing us. The traffic, the pollution. We prefer this downsized life. I can actually breathe. See the stars. Walk to the beach. When I'm here on my ancestor's land, I feel at home."

As if on cue, a strong breeze wafts through this sandy hill. I can see the ocean on the horizon. Patsy, meanwhile, squeezes the oranges with her bare hands at the picnic table.

"Did you see Taylor Ogura's story on Wynn Hightower?" I ask Alice.

"Oh, everyone's been texting us about that. I think it will help with the resistance." Alice talks as if she's in a real-life Hunger Games world.

The old sugarcane plants rustle for a bit until the bruddah who I saw at the protest emerges. He wears a yellow tank top and a bandanna around his neck. His face and clothing are streaked with sweat.

Alice makes the introduction. "This is Pono Akau. He's been leading the resistance."

"She's the one who got arrested first at Hightower's hotel in Poʻipū," Patsy explains as she places a glass with orange juice in my chair's cup holder.

He presses his forehead into mine and breathes out a ceremonial "ha" to give me a proper greeting among warriors, and I feel like a fraud. More than the ʻāina, the land,

I care about my father.

"Yes, we need more sistahs like you out dea."

"I've seen you on YouTube," I tell him.

"Been fighting dis ting for years. Last year it was burial sites around here." The fluffy tops of the sugarcane plants nod in the wind. "So where you from?"

"Waimea," I tell him.

"We had one bruddah from Waimea who wen come to one of our early meetings."

"Really? Who?" Waimea is so small, most of the original residents know one another.

"Lemme see. What was his name? His 'ohana has claim to da 'āina here. But he gone after da first meeting. Don't know what happened to him."

Before we can exchange more personal information, a huge bruddah, almost the size of Patsy, pushes a slight figure forward from the sugarcane fields. He says, "Look, we got one haole spy here." It's Sean, who looks more annoyed than scared. "He was taking photos of everyting, like he workin' for Hightower."

I get up from the camping chair. "Oh, no, he's not one spy. He's my friend. He drove me here."

"Dis your driver? He no look like one driver."

"Well, I drive but technically I'm not haole," Sean says to the bruddah. *What is he doing?*

"So whatchu den, hapa haole?" Pono asks.

"I'm Jewish."

"Jewish." Both Pono and his friend, whose name is Kai Calistro, ponder that for a moment.

"Lots of Jews in Los Angeles," Patsy comments. *Not helpful.*

"He's a Nazi hunter," I blurt out.

"What?" Pono seems intrigued.

Sean explains that 10,000 Nazi collaborators entered the US illegally after World War II. He's been on the search for a specific war criminal, John Fischer, who is hiding out in Hawai'i, maybe specifically on Kaua'i.

"His grandfather was a Holocaust survivor," I pipe in, thinking that it will make an impact.

It does. Pono's face loses its hard edge. "I hope you find him. If you need mo' help, let me know."

I change the subject back to why I'm here. "Hightower has to be stopped."

"We will," Pono says. "We have some friends in the traditional media now, plus we can take our message straight to the people through YouTube."

"No, I mean, we can do things to him."

Pono frowns. "Like what dat bruddah did to Luke Hightower at dat shave ice place? Santiago's?"

"Hold on, isn't that what your name is?" Alice interrupts. "Leilani Santiago."

I feel my cheeks burn.

Pono's eyes flash. "You da daughter. Whatchu doing hea?"

"Maybe she has a police wire," Kai says.

"No, I not trying for trap you or da kine," I say. This conversation is taking a terrible turn.

"Sistah," Pono says as he unties the bandanna around his neck. "I tink it's time you went back to Waimea."

I feel like a fool as Sean and I make our way to the parking lot. Between the Hightowers and the "resistance," I still

haven't learned anything new. Only that the Hightowers
have the most beautiful garden that I've seen in my life, and
that Patsy squeezes some excellent orange juice. Nothing
that will prove my father's innocence or lead us to Luke's
real killer.

I want to go back to Waimea as quickly as possible,
but someone is standing in front of Sean's parked van. "Go
ahead," I motion to Sean to get in the driver's seat. I will
handle Celia Johnson.

"I thought that I saw you go onto our property." Celia
has straightened her hair since I last saw her. It shimmers
like a gold waterfall in the sun. Damn her.

"That's not your property. That's kuleana land," I tell
her. "Besides, I don't think any of this is yours."

"Well, this is Wynn's property." She extends her arms
from the parking lot to Bamboo Royal.

"Well, get out of the way and we'll leave."

She doesn't move. "So were you behind it, that article in
the paper this morning?"

"How can I be? I know nothing about law. Learned
about quiet title from the story."

"The timing is sure suspicious," she says. We go back
and forth and she continues to insult me. But I'm a former
volleyball defensive specialist, a DS. I've been trained to respond to any kind of attack.

Before our words can escalate to anything physical, Rex
appears. When I first met him, I thought he was kind of
cute, but now he seems so gutless and weak. A total turnoff.

"What's going on?" he asks.

I cut to the chase. "Did you know she was sleeping with
Luke's father?"

His neck reddens, but he says nothing, as if he's trying

to figure out how to respond.

"Dammit, you knew! But you didn't have the balls to tell Luke. Is it because his father was your financial sponsor?"

"Shut up, you bitch!" Celia begins screaming at me, loud enough for other guests at the B&B to open up the windows of their room. Sean starts to get out of the van, but I have had enough. "Let's go." And we do.

"You mind if we make a stop in Kapa'a?" Sean asks as he steers the van down a dirt road in Moloa'a Valley.

"What's up?"

"The dealer your dad sold the surfboard to. He's willing to see me if you come with."

"Why me?"

"I guess he trusts your family. He said he met you a couple of times when you were in elementary school. Ronaldo West."

"My dad sold the surfboard to Ronaldo West?" What the heck? Ronaldo West is more of a wheeler-dealer than a legitimate businessman. He's a junk man and pawnbroker who used to travel around in a beat-up old camper. I'd heard he had a real office/apartment, but my mom never encouraged me to accompany my father on any visits.

"I can't believe that Ronaldo had the fifteen grand to even give my father in the first place," I tell Sean.

"Well, he must have had a ready buyer."

Ronaldo does know all the eccentrics and hoarders on Kaua'i, because he is both of those himself. I fear what we will find in Kapa'a.

Old Kapa'a Town is for tourists. There's an innovative shave ice place there that always ends up on the "Best of" lists. As we pass by, I think that Santiago's needs to up its game. I know Baachan is going to protest, but we need to employ more high-tech, get a Square reader for credit cards and a website. And the flavors—we need to take advantage of all the natural fruit that Kaua'i offers.

Ronaldo's place is not in Old Kapa'a. It's west of there, in a residential area that has the same vibe as our neighborhood. Little bungalows with small yards, except most of these in Kapa'a are built off the ground because it's wetter here. Sean finally stops the van in front of a gray unit that has a plumbing truck parked in the driveway. Has Uncle Ronaldo diversified his services?

"Are you sure it's here?" I ask Sean.

He rechecks his phone. "This is the address he gave me."

We both get out of the van cautiously. There's a beat of music reverberating from the front room. Somebody is home.

The doorbell is useless, so Sean bangs on the metal security gate. First a little tentatively and then full force. We can hear swearing, and finally the door swings open. Through the bars we see a bruddah who is completely tatted up, even his face.

"Yeah?"

"Who the hell is it?" A scrawny bruddah with a shaved head joins him at the door.

Both men ignore Sean and fixate on me. They give me a good once-over and I pull at my T-shirt, wishing that I had worn an XL instead of a large.

"We're here to see Ronaldo West." Sean's voice sounds so thin competing against the rap music.

"Ronaldo? He lives out back," the face tat says.

"You can walk through our place." The skinny one gives me a special invitation and swings open the metal gate.

"No, we'll just go from the driveway." Sean tries to shield me from the leering men. Unfortunately, it's something I've gotten used to over the years.

In the backyard is a makeshift tiny house, barely 200 square feet. I've seen those tiny homes on home-improvement TV shows and websites, but no one would do a TV show on this one. It's built on wheels, mostly in totan, what we call our corrugated steel. It seems completely jerry-rigged with junkyard materials. Yup, this would be Uncle Ronaldo's place. Next to the house is an open shed, filled with stacks of traditional artwork like wood tikis and also boxes of HDTV flat screens. As we get close to the house, the door, barely hanging on to its frame, swings open.

"A-lo-ha!" Uncle Ronaldo looks as grizzled as ever with a salt and pepper beard and full head of hair. "My, you've really grown up, Leilani."

I don't like his tone and wonder if I might be safer with the two bruddahs inside the main house. "Hi, Uncle."

"Come into my humble abode."

We go up some steps covered with flattened rubber from tires. The house has big windows in the back, bringing welcomed light to the minuscule space. Ronaldo has hung nets from the ceiling that hold a strange assortment of goods: giant dried gourds used by traditional Hawaiian dancers, autographed footballs, boogie boards, and old brown McDonald's trays. In the main area is a small card table, where an old desktop computer rests with a pile of paperwork and a basket filled with thumbnail drives. Ronaldo pulls down two Japanese beer crates stacked in a corner and pads them with two mismatched soiled zabuton.

"Sit, sit," he says while plopping down in an ergonomic chair on rollers that's missing one arm.

Do I have to? I think, as I gingerly place my okole on one of the zabuton.

"I don't get many visitors. Most of customers prefer communicating via the World Wide Web."

I wonder why.

Sean speaks up. "I mentioned that I was interested in the surfboard that Mr. Santiago sold to you."

"Oh, yes, yes. Sorry, brah, that's already sold. But I can get you another surfboard from the 1920s." Ronaldo puts on some reading glasses and starts clicking on his keyboard.

"No, I want that specific one. Can you give me the buyer's contact information?"

Ronaldo examines Sean over his glasses. "Nah, I can't do that. I keep my client's names confidential, you know."

"Uncle, can't you make an exception?" I intervene. "My dad is the one who got the surfboard for you in the first place."

Ronaldo huffs and puffs, and finally Sean brings out a folded bill, revealing half of Benjamin Franklin's face.

"Would this help?" Sean slides the bill to Ronaldo.

"Hmm, well, well." The bill disappears in Ronaldo's fist. He returns to his computer. "The thing is, you can't tell this guy how you got his contact information. He likes his privacy." Ronaldo jots down something on a yellow Post-it, peels it from the stack, and hands it to Sean.

"Thank you."

"Mahalo, Uncle."

I can't wait to leave Ronaldo's tiny house. As I head for the door, I remember that Ronaldo had been the one who'd been in Waimea Junction early Sunday morning to collect the surfboard. I ask whether he recalls anything out of the ordinary that day.

Ronaldo tips his head back and strokes his chin whiskers. "The back door was wide open to your shave ice place. Figured you forgot to lock it, so I closed it, just to be safe. Who knew that a dead surfer would be inside?"

Once we're back in the van, we look at the information written on the Post-it. Just a first name, Chris, an email address, and a snail-mail address in Kekaha, a town west of Waimea.

"Do you think that it could be him?"

"Not sure. Either way, I'm curious why someone would spend so much money on a surfboard with a swastika on it."

I get chicken skin from thinking that I may have been waiting in a grocery store line behind someone who had been involved in something so horrible.

"What are you going to do if you find him?"

"Report him to the authorities. There's no statute of limitations on war criminals."

Sean's passion spurs me in my own mission to free my father. I think back to what Pono said. That a bruddah from Waimea has secret connections to the land around Bamboo Royal. Could he be talking about Kelly and Pekelo, the Kahuakai brothers? I shudder, pulling at my seat belt. I may be uncovering some family secrets of people I'm closest to.

Once we get closer to Waimea Junction, I ask Sean to drop me off at Santiago's.

"Mahalo fo' everyting," I tell him. "And good luck with your hunt."

He smiles. "Good luck to both of us."

Baachan is napping on her corner perch inside of Santiago's. How she can sleep sitting up is beyond me.

"Baachan!" I call out, and she finally blinks herself awake.

"Yah?"

"Where's Dad and Mom?"

"They went to meet with some lawyer in Līhu'e. Recommended by Emily's professor. Judge says Tommy can travel for dat."

I feel immediately relieved. Maybe this lawyer will be the answer to our problems. I glance at our trash can. It's practically empty. Did we have any customers today?

"Hardly anybody came," Baachan confirms. "Dat girl wen do da Facebooky ting and tell people for stay away."

When I hear "girl" and "Facebooky," I know immediately who Baachan is talking about. I look up Celia's Facebook page and sure enough, she did a Facebook Live video around the time we left Bamboo Royal. "I would encourage everyone—tourists and the good people of Kaua'i—to boycott Santiago's, who is harboring a killer."

It has more than 200 likes and has been shared thirty-six, now thirty-seven, times.

Shit.

"Baachan, I'll be next door at Killer Wave," I tell her, but she's already nodded back to sleep.

The two brothers are working today, which makes it all the more convenient. "Is dea someting you two not tellin' me?"

Kelly is hanging up some wet suits, while Pekelo is at a desk.

"Howzit, Leilani?" Kelly says. He doesn't pick up the angry tone of my voice.

I'm in no mood for "howzit" or "aloha." None of this sweet-Kelly bullshit. "No ack Kelly. I'm sick of it!"

Kelly nearly drops the merchandise that he's handling. "What's wrong?"

"Your 'ohana has ties to kuleana land where Mr. High-tower wants to build."

"You mento," Kelly says. One thing about Kelly is that he cannot lie. At least not well. I can tell that he's telling the truth now.

We both look at Pekelo, who seems transfixed by something he's reading on his laptop.

"I wen meet wid da resistance bruddahs. They told me you went to one meeting." I toss out a fishing line to see if Pekelo bites.

He continues to sit there, typing away on his keyboard as if I hadn't said a thing.

"Pekelo, you wen hear me. And you met with Mr. Hightower da day before Luke arrived."

"Huh?" Kelly first seems confused, but he knows his brother. Something is up. "Pekelo?"

Pekelo takes a deep breath. "Yah, it's true." He confirms that the Kahuakai family has kuleana land near Bamboo Royal Hills.

"Why you nevah say notting?"

"I try for make one deal with Wynn. Gonna sell him da land."

"So you on one first-name basis wid him?" The wet suits fall to the ground as Kelly approaches his brother. "I'm your only blood. How come you wen hide'um from me?"

Pekelo's jaw tightens.

"You always tell me da 'āina is everyting," Kelly says.

"Well, I was wrong. I went thousands of miles to fight for people's land. And you know what, I not sure was worth it."

"You not tinking straight."

"Maybe not. But more than da 'āina, I care for you, my

lil bruddah. Our future. We have no future here, workin' for
Leilani's father. You gonna be a married man. Don't you
need money for a new life?"

"We not selling. Dat's Kahuakai 'ohana 'āina."

"You pupule," Pekelo insults Kelly. "You makin' one big
mistake. Mr. Hightower offering both of us one chance to
get off dis island. And you are trowing it away."

Chapter Fourteen

I WALK TEN STEPS BEHIND Baachan the whole way from Santiago's back to the house.

Finally Baachan stops and bears her fist down on her weak hip.

"Wassamattayou? Slowpoke."

I try to quicken my steps, but it's like all my energy has been pushed out of my body. I didn't mean for the two Kahuakai brothers to war with each other, but that's what happened. Kelly stormed out of Killer Wave, leaving me alone with Pekelo, who gave me big stink eye. "See whatchu did, Leilani."

"Pekelo says that I so niele, dat I put my nose into things I shouldn't," I confess to Baachan.

"Eh, if he telling da truth, den no problem." Maybe Baachan knows what's going on more than I think. At least I didn't straight out accuse Pekelo of being Luke's killer. If I did that, our friendship would most likely be irreparably damaged.

I drag myself up the hill to our house. The screen door is closed, but the front door is open. I half expect to see Mom and Dad sitting on our love seat in the living room, but instead it's someone else with his bare feet up on our coffee table.

"Uncle Rick?" Duke is also in the house and comes up from the floor to greet me.

"Now a dog, too?" Baachan shakes her head at our growing menagerie of animals. She's so upset that she barely acknowledges Rick and instead disappears into her bedroom.

"Waitin' for your dad. I going stay da night." Rick sits up. His face is pasty-looking, with red splotches on his forehead and cheeks.

"Eh." I play with Duke a bit and rub his stomach. I sit on the floor, waiting to hear what's going on.

"I left Barbara," he says. "It was too hard. I was staying sober and she was just bringing me down."

I feel both weird and honored to listen to his adult problems. Something has shifted in our relationship. He doesn't see me as a little girl anymore.

"Auntie Barbara has been drinkin', too." I say it to convince myself of it.

Rick nods. "You notice?"

"Sophie was actually da one to say."

Rick drops his head in shame. Sometimes it takes a twelve-year-old to see the plain truth. "Your dad's been helping me through it. I didn't want to leave Barbara, but he convinced me dat's da only way she can get betta herself."

"Whatchu gonna do?"

"Haven't figured out my next step. May go Honolulu where my bruddah lives."

"We'll miss you. Dad, especially."

That night Baachan and I make curry rice from a package. All of us, including Uncle Rick, eat until the bottom of our pots are shiny clean. We say nothing of Rick and Barbara's problems or my parents' meeting with the lawyer and laugh when Duke stays under the table and licks our toes for any spilled leftovers. We are a house full of problems and brokenness, but we choose not to dwell on that for one night.

"So how did the meeting with the lawyer go?" I ask Mom the next morning. The girls are at school, and Dad and Rick are in the backyard attempting to build a chicken coop, much to the consternation of Baachan. Duke is out there, too, chasing Jimin and the neighborhood cats that wander into our yard.

"She seems to be pretty sharp. She actually worked in the Honolulu public defender's office before coming out here to start her own practice. She says the DA has a weak case. No one saw Daddy do it, and no one even saw him in Waimea that night."

Could our luck be turning?

"Only thing is," she says and takes a sip of her green smoothie. "She's expensive. But I'm trying not to think about that. Hope that everything moves fast so we don't have to keep paying for the lawyer."

"How about the shave ice mold?"

Mom shakes her head. "I don't know if it got wet in the rain, but there were no fingerprints."

Damn. Here I thought that I'd made a groundbreaking discovery.

Mom must have read the disappointment on my face because she pats my hand. "It was good for you to try. That's da main thing: We can't give up."

It looks like another slow day at Santiago's. Baachan and I made a pact not to tell my parents about Celia's "Face-booky," but I'm worried. While Dad might be saved by the lawyer, we may be killed by her high prices.

"Oh, my God, Leilani, one big mess." Court, wearing her work apron, walks into Santiago's. She has a Disney bandage around her index finger—one of the hazards of working with sharp implements. "They are not talking to each other. Kelly says that he's no like Pekelo be his best man anymore."

"I'm so sorry," I say. "My bad. I should have nevah brought it up."

"And let Pekelo sell the family land without getting Kelly's permission? Dat's da worst."

I'm relieved that Court doesn't blame me.

"Since we talkin' about it, I wanna ask you—will you be my maid of honor?"

"What do I have to do?"

"Well, plan a bridal shower."

No problem.

"And wear a dress. I know dat you no like fru-fru stuff. It may have lace."

I swallow. I think I'm emotionally allergic to lace. "For you, Court, I will do it for you."

"And maybe wear false eyelashes."

"Court!"

"Actually, forget da false eyelashes. I no like you lookin' betta than me."

"What?"

"Leilani, if you only realized. . . ."

I forget that Baachan has been sitting there, listening to our whole conversation. She lets out a honk that would

rival any nēnē, Hawaiian goose, I've ever heard. "You wearin'
one lace dress. I betta live long enough to see dat."

Business is so slow that I tell Baachan to go home. I use this
time to make Santiago's spic and span. I start with our shave
ice machine. We bought this one after my freshman year at
UW. Our old one broke down so we had to get a loan to
replace it. As this new one produced the finest, smoothest
shave ice, business immediately went up and our Yelp reviews improved. Just think if we made more upgrades.

    I clean the main counter by our pop-up window and do
inventory on our syrups. A shave ice truck in Old Kapaʻa
Town uses fresh fruits like papaya and pineapple. What if
we did the same, starting with fruit from our own mango
tree? That's something Mom could get into.

    Next I go into our pantry and check the canned goods.
We are running low on the red beans—the beans that
Baachan loves so much. They are expensive, so I don't want
to order too many of them. There's plenty of sweetened
condensed milk and li hing mui powder packages. Not so
much matcha powder, but that's pricey, too. And in our
freezer, we have enough Dole Whip. Since we don't have
a self-serve machine, we just mix water with a package and
put it into the freezer. Probably next on our "to buy" list
should be a self-serve ice cream machine, but I know that
I'm way ahead of myself. First order of business: Make sure
Dad doesn't go to jail, we don't lose our house, and Mom
stays healthy.

    Most customers just order at the window, but occa-
sionally people besides my family come through our front

door. Usually it's confused customers—toddlers, old people, or folks from foreign countries—who don't know better. I'm cleaning the metal tips of our syrup bottles when the door opens and closes.

"This is your business?" Celia the witch has returned on her broom.

"What are you doing here? Plenty of shave ice places in the North Shore."

She surveys our small dingy working place. Even with me doing a thorough cleaning, Santiago's is unimpressive. "You live such a sad life," she comments.

"What do you want?" I don't need any more trouble from Celia and her Facebook Live reports.

"I need that photo back. The photo that you showed Wynn. If you give it back, I'll call off the boycott."

Blackmail. Is that her regular MO?

If I can't get Celia easily out of Santiago's, I can try to ignore her. The tip to our root beer syrup bottle is crusty, I notice. Not a popular flavor. I've told Sophie that we need to get rid of it, but she fights me on it, insisting that it is essential for her signature flavor, Blue Monster.

"Wynn's suffering, too. We're all suffering."

Cue the violins.

"We're really in love."

I wonder if Mrs. Hightower has been informed of this.

"Luke was too soft. Too romantic. We weren't serious, at least I didn't think he was. We were working on the sponsorship and one thing led to another. He told everyone that we were boyfriend and girlfriend."

I stop cleaning and think for a moment. "You were already seeing his father."

"It turned out to be convenient. If I was with Luke, I

could be close to Wynn, too."

"I can't see Mr. Hightower being happy about this arrangement."

"There wasn't much that Wynn could say."

A lightbulb comes on in my mind. "Because of Mrs. Hightower." For Celia, Luke was a bargaining chip. As long as Wynn stayed with his wife, Celia would be with Luke. Rich and beautiful people are so *kitanai*, Baachan's Japanese word for dirty.

"Wynn came early to Kaua'i to be with me before Luke showed up."

"So when were you going to tell Luke about your relationship?"

"I hadn't thought that far."

Did Wynn Hightower fall into a jealous rage about his son being with his young mistress? Or was he sick enough that he didn't care?

Celia gets a sense of where my mind is going. "I can guarantee that Wynn didn't kill Luke. After you came by Bamboo Royal that Saturday night, I went to his house in Hanalei. He was with me all night, and I mean all night."

"You're Wynn Hightower's alibi. And he's yours. Why should anyone believe you? You both could have come here that night."

"There are security cameras all over his property that feed into a central system. Anyone can check to see exactly when we each arrived. And when we left."

I'm sure those could be doctored.

"Neither one of us wanted to see Luke dead." Celia steps into the exact place where I found Luke's body. If she had killed him, would she even dare to return to the scene of the crime? Was she that much of a stone-cold killer?

Tears run down her cheeks, and a part of me wants to laugh.

"Here," I finally say. "What's your phone number?" She eagerly gives it to me and I text her the photo. "And look, see, I'm deleting it from my phone." I even show her that I'm doing it. Nori and Taylor Ogura still have it, so I'm actually relieved to remove such filth from my device.

"Thank you," she says. "I'll call off the boycott. Do you want to be in a selfie?"

I decline. "Do me one last favor."

"What?"

"Don't ever step into our business again."

After Celia leaves, it's quiet again at Santiago's. It doesn't seem peaceful, however. I hate to admit it, but I think Celia is telling the truth. I've experienced that first rush of love—or maybe it's more lust—when you are so blinded that you can't see the person you are sleeping with honestly. I don't know what it is about Wynn Hightower. He's certainly not bad looking for his age, but money, power, and experience must have won Celia over. And Mrs. Hightower? Who knows what her deal is? How can she spend her life with a dirtbag like her husband? Or maybe she's hanging in there for her children—now only her daughter?

I'm full of thoughts when the door opens again. This time it's Sean. I get a tingly feeling in my body and I immediately shake it off. We greet each other and I give him the latest on my father's case. "My parents found a lawyer. A good one, I think. Someone my sister's law professor recommended. But thanks for your referrals. I really appreciate it."

Sean nods. His cheeks are a bit ruddy from either the sun or excitement. "I wanted to tell you that I went there—

to Kekaha."

"You mean to see the guy who bought the surfboard?"

Sean nods. "It turned out to be a retired finance guy, a surfer. He's a collector, like you predicted."

I don't feel any joy in being right. "I'm sorry. I know that you really want to find John Fischer."

"Yeah." Sean pauses and grins. "And get this—the guy's Jewish."

"No way."

We both share a laugh.

"You busy? I wanted to show you some things I'm doing in my space."

Since it's so slow, I close up the window and put up the "We'll be back" sign on our door.

I hadn't noticed that Sean has made renovations to his space. He's created a sitting area in the front, with low bookshelves underneath the window. "That's for the books. 'Books and Suds.'"

"You can't be serious." I'm both stunned and honored that he really considered my concept.

"We have a nice library right here in Waimea, so I figure I'll specialize. Mostly used books. Maybe business, science, history, and mysteries."

"Mysteries are my favorite," I tell him. "But don't forget about handcrafts like stitching and quilting. Lotta folks like my mom are into that."

He makes a note of that and continues with the tour. In the back of the space are drying racks, and by the sink is a giant pot that swings on a metal frame. "That's where we mix the soap," he explains.

I look around. "Isn't making soap kinda dangerous? You need chemicals, eh?"

"Lye—I haven't brought any in yet. But once you mix the essential oils with the lye and cure the loaves of soap, the lye is all used up. Gone."

"Hmm," I say. "Sounds interesting. I want to watch you make it."

"I'll let you know. Maybe we can cross-promote. I can think of ingredients to make Leilani soap."

A soap named after me? I am overwhelmed and make some excuse that I have to go back to work. A couple of people are standing outside the shack, and I'm thankful that we actually have customers. Celia must have issued her ceasefire announcement on social media.

Still, there are lulls through the early afternoon. I continue my cleaning crusade. After tackling the main room, I go into the back kitchen. Our icebox is pretty empty, but there are old leftovers in there from the luau. All that goes straight to the trash can. Underneath the table is the makeshift "Lost and Found" box that Pekelo made after I found Luke. Trash, trash, trash. I notice one thing that shouldn't be there. Then it becomes completely clear to me. I know who killed Luke Hightower.

Chapter Fifteen

I SEND A SIMPLE TEXT:

You left something at Santiago's.

There's no response back. I don't expect one. I text Sammie and tell her that she doesn't have to come in today. She's completely fine with that. All I can do is wait.

The sun breaks through the clouds and it begins to get warm. A rush of middle-school kids flock to Santiago's. "What color you want?" I ask them one by one. I recognize a few of Sophie's classmates, wealthier ones who have an extra three, four dollars that they can pay for this kind of treat.

The door opens and closes. I look away from the blinding sun, and it takes me a few moments for my eyesight to adjust to the inside darkness.

"You said that I left something." Barbara's face is more pale than usual. I wonder if she's like Emily, whose skin loses color when she drinks.

"Hello, Auntie," I say.

I close our pop-up window and turn on the light. I bring the "Lost and Found" box to the counter. I've left only one item in there, a red scrunchie. This hair accessory is no ordinary one because it has some embroidery on it. A black Labrador in honor of Duke. My mother made it for Auntie Barbara in February for her birthday. Barbara hasn't been at Santiago's except for the recent luau. Yet this scrunchie was on the floor where Luke Hightower's body lay.

Normally, I wouldn't be afraid to be alone with Auntie Barbara, who, in fact, is wearing her hair back in a scrunchie. She was like a member of the family. The way she looks right now sends shivers down my spine. Maybe I should have told someone before alerting Barbara on my own.

"Eh, I lookin' for my scrunchie." Barbara slurs her words a little. "Must have left it at the luau. Tanks, so special to me." As she reaches for the scrunchie, I move the box away from her.

"You didn't leave it at the luau. You left it when you killed Luke Hightower. Right here, in this room."

Barbara's eyes get big, and she puts her arms out as if she is trying to maintain her balance.

"You thought Luke was my father. They were both wearing those baka glow-in-the-dark Killer Wave shirts. So you got one of the ices and clubbed him with it. In the exact spot that it would hurt him the most." With her knowledge of living things, she probably knows where humans are most physically vulnerable.

"No, nevah happen like dat."

"You owe me, Auntie Barbara. You're like family. You know what hell we've been goin' through. I deserve an answer. Why did you do this? And why did you keep it quiet?"

My words stoke a fire under Barbara. "Rick is my everyting. And your faddah was telling him to leave me. Dat both of us would be better separate." She walks toward me. There's a glint from something in her right hand. Her keys, which I know is attached to a folding knife.

I take a few steps back. I feel my throat closing up and heat rising up to the top of my head. *Breathe, Leilani, breathe*, I tell myself.

I put my hand in my back pocket and feel the surface of my phone. I touch some random numbers. I'm calling someone, but I don't know who. If they pick up, I hope that they hear what is happening.

"I don't want to hurt you, Auntie Barbara, and I know that you don't want to hurt me. Tell the police what happened. You drunk, so you don't know whatchu doin'."

She starts to replay that night as if she needs to confess. "I waited for Tommy. Seemed like hours. Then somebody wen come in from da back. Then I knew I couldn't wait. I came from behind and he dropped, so easy like dat."

Still clutching at her keys, she tells me about all the pain and loneliness that she is going through. "You still young. You have no idea."

If I scream and yell, someone is bound to hear me, right?

The door opens. My father is in the doorway. And behind him is Sean, his glasses reflecting the ceiling light. "I've called the police," he announces.

"Barbara, you want me. Not Leilani. I'm here. You come afta me," my dad says.

Barbara turns, still wobbling.

I feel sick. I hate seeing my auntie like this. She's much better than this.

"You wen ruin my life," she says.

Another person pushes my father aside. "Barbara, please," Rick extends his arms. "It's all ova now."

Sergeant Toma and Andy have arrived, and this time Auntie Barbara's hands are secured with wrist ties. I think that

I've now experienced a lifetime of arrests. It's okay on *Law & Order*, but I don't need to see any more for a long while or maybe forever.

"Well, I guess you'll get your bail money back," Toma says to me and my father.

Thank God, I think, but Dad sneers. "Not always about money," he comments and walks out the back door.

We stand near the recycle shed, where there's still some trash from the luau. I don't think Dad can bear to see Barbara be carted out to the patrol car.

"Did you suspect that it was Auntie Barbara?" I ask him.

"Thought it could have been her." He explains that he thought she was eavesdropping on his private conversation with Rick. And later he told both of them that he was going to return to Waimea Junction to take care of some business. "But I wasn't gonna tell da police anyting."

"You might have gone to jail for her."

My dad shakes his head. "If I went to jail, it was for Luke. I was supposed to take care of him, but I nevah."

Later on, Dad tells Rick that he can still stay with us, but Rick declines. "Dat's too uncomfortable." And none of us try to convince him otherwise. Mama Liu comes by to take Rick and Duke back to the North Shore. "I got chickens to take care of," he says, and I know Dad fears that he may start drinking again. This is when I think of what Travis kept reminding me: *We can't take responsibility for someone else's bad decisions.* I don't dare to say that out loud, but it's a wonder that it comes to haunt me tonight.

Chapter Sixteen

"YOU ALREADY 'WAKE?" Baachan comes into the kitchen without her dentures. She takes a big sniff. "Smells like rice."

She's followed by Sophie and Dani, their bare feet making slapping noises against the linoleum.

"You okay, Leilani?" Dani asks.

"Ta-da!" I show them what I've been working on for the past hour. Stacks of musubi: some triangular ones with *umeboshi*, red pickled plum, inside, others with tuna mayo, and smaller ones covered in furikake. And, of course, squares of Spam musubi.

"I made you and Ro a special lunch." I throw half a dozen of them in a paper bag.

"And you, too, Dani." She gets three *umeboshi* ones because that's her favorite.

"One *obake* take ova your body?" Baachan is mystified.

"It was a joint effort," Mom says, returning back to the kitchen. "Girls, get your backpacks and hurry on to school."

"So what? You want Kona coffee?" Baachan, her dentures now in her mouth, says as she measures out some ground coffee beans into the drip machine "Or you gonna drink your hi-tone kine from Seattle?" I actually have already taken both those beans to Santiago's for an experiment, but don't want to reveal that now.

"You know what? I think I may have half-and-half. Mix it up."

Baachan raises her sparse eyebrows. "Eh, now you talkin'."

Our spirits have been lifted since Dad's murder charges were dropped. His ankle bracelet was removed and our bail money returned. The Līhu'e attorney was thanked but told her services were not needed. I even called Travis to tell him the good news. At first his voice was so cold that I immediately regretted calling him, but at the end of our conversation he says, "Thanks for letting me know. I've been wondering what happened."

Of course, with good news also come bad. We all felt bad for Auntie Barbara, especially Mom. She was the one who had helped personalize the key piece of evidence, the embroidered scrunchie. "Tommy shouldn't have gone so hard after her," she said to Mama Liu, who'd stopped by to pick up the cleaver we had borrowed from her months ago.

"Dat's bulai," Mama Liu said. "She wen try for kill Tommy, remember? Now one innocent boy dead."

Other evidence piled up against Auntie Barbara. A witness reported a driver under the influence crashing into a railing near Kapa'a that Saturday night. The paint matched the scrape on Auntie Barbara's car. I still can't believe that she was able to drive all the way to Santiago's in that state. It just shows how scared she was to lose Uncle Rick. Now he's definitely by her side through all of this. And, of course, since she's in jail, she's sober. In a weird and terribly ironic turn of events, the Chens ended up with what they wanted. Aside for Luke Hightower being the sacrificial lamb.

Over my coffee and her kale juice, I tell Mom that I've been contemplating my future.

"Don't rush, Leilani. Think about what you really want." Her skin doesn't look so papery thin this morning.

"Santiago's going to be all right without you. Baachan and I can keep it going. Sammie says she can work more hours and D-man will help, too."

A part of me feels the sting of not being so needed. But that's what my mom always had told me. When it comes to work, no one is irreplaceable. In terms of being someone's mother, that's a whole other story.

"No, I want to be here," I tell her. "Really. Maybe not a few months ago. But I have some ideas for Santiago's."

"Ambitious," Mom says to me, breaking out in a smile. "Your father would be happy to hear about that."

"By the way, I have a special announcement to make. Since the girls have only a half day of school, can you bring them ova to Santiago's afterward? Dad and Baachan, too?"

At first Mom seems worried, like what's going to happen next? But we Santiagos have come this far. If we are together, we can get through anything.

I've barely opened the shack for five minutes when Court barges in, her hands full of magazines. She puts them down on our counter.

"What are these?" I ask.

"Bridal catalogs."

Aisus! She can sense that I'm less than thrilled. She comes up to me and places a lei over my neck. "And here's a leftover lei to make the reading go down better."

"Gee, mahalo." I have to admit that it smells magnificent.

She leans back into the counter. I know that she wants to talk story. "They still not talkin' to each other. Kelly says he can't forgive him."

Maybe the two brothers need some time to cool down, I suggest.

"Pekelo's moved into the garden shed."

"Fo' real?"

"That shed ready for come down. Also a lot of poison stored in there, right? He took it all out and put it in the garage. I think that he might try for build one sink or even a benjo out there."

"What, fo' real?" Sounds like Ronaldo West–style living.

"Yah, fo' real." She spots my experiment on one side of the counter. "What dis, anyway?"

My three Mason jars of cold-brew coffee. "My experiment. Come try latah."

"I wish. Gotta make a delivery to Kapaʻa." She lingers. I know something else is on her mind.

"What?"

"A part of me feels relieved Pekelo's in the shed because I'm supposed to move in the house once we married. Dat's so bad, eh?" Court covers her face with her perfectly manicured fingers.

"No," I say, "you human."

Around one o'clock, Mom comes around with Baachan, Dani, and Sophie. Sophie's talking a mile a minute about some new gossip about Jimin—the performer, not the rooster. Dani, the visual one, notices the new addition to the chalkboard, but I put my index finger to my lips to signal for her to keep my secret.

"When's Dad coming?" I ask.

"He's on his way," Mom assures me.

"What dis all about?" Baachan asks.

"What, you have someting bettah to go to?"

Baachan sneers at me and I sneer right back at her. We indeed have a special relationship.

I look out our pop-out window for Dad. Instead I spot Sean walking through the parking lot.

"Come in, come in," I say to him. "Perfect timing. I have an announcement to make."

When he enters, the whole family, even Baachan, crowd around him. I think that Baachan may have a crush on him. How can I break it to her that he's about fifty years her junior?

Sean is eventually able to break free from the adoring female Santiagos and make his way to me. "I'm thinking of having monthly tenant meetings," he says. "You know, so we can brainstorm and think of ways of getting more people to come to Waimea."

"Meetings?" I'm more allergic to meetings than lace.

"Parties, then?"

I nod. Sean Cohen may become a Hawai'i boy yet.

Dad finally wanders into the shack. He looks lost, and I have a feeling why. Luke's paddle-out in San Clemente is happening about now.

I stand behind the Mason jars on the counter and whistle to get everyone's attention. Now is the time for my announcement. "Well, most of you all know this, but I'm a coffee freak."

I explain to everyone that I've made cold-brew coffee with three ground beans from different locations: Seattle, Kona, and finally Kaua'i. The beans and cold water have sat overnight in separate Mason jars. I strain each one of them in cheesecloth and now the testing begins.

I shave about a cup of ice in multiple bowls, topping

them with sweetened condensed milk, bits of almonds, and the cold-brew coffee. We take turns tasting each one.

"Hey, dis is barely notting," Sophie exclaims at the small amount of coffee ice that I've placed in her and Dani's bowls.

"Coffee is supposed to stunt your growth. You don't want to be a real-life menehune, do you?"

Sophie sticks her tongue out at me and I stick mine back at her. We have a special relationship, too.

"This one is the best," Sean points to the third bowl. Everyone else nods in agreement. The local beans. Pretty convenient, and it's always good to go local.

"Well, this is my signature flavor." I point to the chalkboard, where I've added "Wake Up, Waimea." "What do all you think?"

"Onolicious," Sean says, practically drinking it from the bowl.

Baachan is the one who pays me the biggest compliment. "I wanna have more."

After celebrating my new signature flavor, the family scatters. When Sammie reports to work, I take out the trash and notice my father walking toward the pier with his surfboard. There are no waves out there, especially at this time. I think that I know what he's up to.

I go into Killer Wave and Kelly is with a family of five, outfitting them with snorkeling gear.

I wave and gesture that I'm going into the back, where one of my wet suits is stored. I change in there and for the hell of it, I keep the wilting lei on me. I borrow a red boogie board and go out the back door.

D-man has arrived, his pickup truck filled with tonight's supplies for the bar.

Once he sees me with the boogie board, he smiles and flashes me a shaka sign.

I throw him one back. No words necessary.

By the time I'm on the beach, Dad's already in the water. He isn't surfing, just sitting on his surfboard, looking toward the horizon.

There are no waves, really, barely any ripples. I kick over next to him.

My father seems surprised to see me. We both bob on our respective boards for a while, watching the clouds pass by.

"I'm sorry, Dad, about Luke." I remove the leftover lei from my neck and hand it over to my father. We don't have to verbally say what this is. It's our own private paddle-out in Waimea for Luke Hightower.

"Yah, he was a good one." He releases the lei—the pearly white tuberose, the brilliant pink Stargazer, the yellow hibiscus—onto the surface of the water. The flowers are like Kaua'i's natural jewels, not destined to last forever but to mark this exact moment with an overwhelming and indelible beauty. My father takes a deep breath of the salt air and I follow. Our breaths are not synchronized. We have our own unique rhythms and beats; one doesn't dominate the other.

We watch as the lei floats toward the sun, and when we can no longer see its colors, we head back home.

THE END

Pidgin (Hawaiian Creole)
and Location Names

I'm not from Hawai'i, but I have been influenced by and exposed to the culture through my life here in California, as well as occasional visits to the Islands. From my college days to working at *The Rafu Shimpo* newspaper, I could not help but be touched by the people and food of Hawai'i.

While I've read many books written in pidgin, I certainly am no expert on this dialect. I've used it sparingly to give the story some authentic flavor. Cynthia Hughes of Honolulu has been a godsend and careful reader and corrector of the pidgin in this mystery. Any errors are mine.

In terms of location names like Hawai'i and Kaua'i, I've chosen to use the okina, which is often mistaken for an apostrophe. The okina indicates a glottal stop in Polynesian languages such as Hawaiian. The University of Hawai'i explains that the okina is "similar to the sound between the syllables of 'oh-oh.'" To respect the origins of the Islands, I've chosen to adopt the use of the okina in names of places and people. The same goes with the kahako, or macron, which indicates the elongation of a vowel sound. I've eliminated both when not included in the use of a proper name, such as Lihue Airport or Kauai Community Correctional Facility.

I've eliminated any italicization of pidgin or Asian-language words commonly used in Hawai'i. However, more unusual words not used in common speech have been italicized.

Select Pidgin, Hawaiian, and Japanese Words in *Iced in Paradise*

(not an inclusive list)

'āina (Hawaiian): land
aisus: shucks, darn it (spoken by Filipinos)
baka (Japanese): stupid
benjo (Japanese): bathroom
bocha: bath, bathe
boro-boro (Japanese): worn-out
broke da mouth: delicious
buggah: guy
bulai: lies, bullshit
chawan (Japanese): rice bowl
chicken skin: goosebumps
dem: them, and others
furikake (Japanese): dry Japanese seasoning, usually with bits
    of nori
grindz: food
hālau (Hawaiian): hula school
hammajang: mess
hanabaddah: snot
hashi (Japanese): chopsticks
haupia (Hawaiian): coconut-based flavor
high makamaka: stuck-up
huhu (Hawaiian): angry, mad
humbug: hassle
imu (Hawaiian): hole or underground oven to roast kalua pig
itadakimasu (Japanese): an expression of thanks said before
    a meal
kine: kind
kuleana (Hawaiian): right or privilege (in the context of
    kuleana land, native Hawaiian land rights)
lolo (Hawaiian): crazy
mahalo (Hawaiian): thank you

menehune (Hawaiian): mythical creature that is small in
    stature
mento: mental, crazy, silly
niele (Hawaiian): nosy, curious
no ack: no act, quit playing around
obake (Japanese): ghost
ogo (Japanese): type of seaweed often used in poke
'ohana (Hawaiian): family
okole (Hawaiian): butt
one: a, the
one oddah: another
ono kau kau: delicious eats
pupule (Hawaiian): crazy
rubbah slippahs: flip-flops
shaka: hang loose hand sign
shibai: drama, lies
shi-shi (Japanese): pee
stick: surfboard
stink eye: dirty looks
talk stink: talk bad about someone
tutu (Hawaiian): grandmother
uji: gross
wen: past tense
yogore (Japanese): dirty
zabuton (Japanese): flat cushion

Recommended Resources and Reading

Lois-Ann Yamanaka's *Wild Meat and the Bully Burgers*
Deb Aoki's Bento Box comic strip
Local Kine Words @localkineapps (Twitter)
Andy Bumatai's "The Daily Pidgin" (YouTube)
Douglas Simonson and Pat Sasaki's *Pidgin to da Max*
Mary Kawena Pukuii and Samuel H. Elbert's *Hawaiian
    Dictionary*

Acknowledgments

First of all, a big mahalo to Prospect Park Books (PPB) publisher Colleen Dunn Bates, who shares my love for Kaua'i and was actually on the island when she first read the beginnings of Leilani's story. Thank you for recognizing that great stories reside in the Hawaiian Islands.

California has many excellent surf museums, and I was able to visit three of them: Surfing Heritage & Culture Center in San Clemente, International Surfing Museum in Huntington Beach; and California Surf Museum in Oceanside. Hal Forsen, one of the preparators at the San Clemente museum, was especially helpful in explaining the development and evolution of surfboards.

Insightful was Gerry Lopez's autobiography, *Surf Is Where You Find It*, especially the sections regarding his personal mixed heritage as well as his relationship with Kaua'i's waves.

For a wider context, I read a number of surf books, including Matt Warshaw's *A Brief History of Surfing* and Ben Finney and James D. Houston's *Surfing: A History of the Ancient Hawaiian Sport*.

In terms of the history of Hawai'i, land rights, and immigration, I can recommend Noenoe K. Silva's *Aloha Betrayed: Native Hawaiian Resistance to American Colonialism*; JoAnna Poblete's *Islanders in the Empire: Filipino and Puerto Rican Laborers in Hawai'i*; and Gary Y. Okihiro's *Cane Fires: The Anti-Japanese Movement in Hawai'i 1865-1945*. Tadashi Nakamura's documentary film, *Mele Murals*, is especially moving and illuminating.

I read numerous articles about quiet title conflicts in Hawai'i in various publications and on websites.

Richard Trank's documentary on Simon Wiesenthal, *I Have Never Forgotten You*, shed light on the commitment of the world-renowned Nazi hunter.

I thank Karlen Kunitomo of Brian's Shave Ice in the Sawtelle District of West Los Angeles for giving me an impromptu tour of her business. Much mahalo.

Librarian Cynthia Chow, who has been a champion of my work in the past, gave me encouragement to tread on her home turf of Hawai'i. And I've mentioned this in the pidgin section, but it's worth it to say again: I'm indebted to a reader, Cynthia Hughes of Honolulu, who reviewed my dialogue and cultural references. The novel is so much better because of Cynthia's input. Also, kudos to Sandra Komo Gauvreau, who is also originally from Hawai'i.

Edwin Ushiro, who did the illustration of Santiago Shave Ice shack on the cover, has inspired me with his artwork related to his home of Hawai'i. In fact, Leilani and the rest of her family and crew really came alive when I perused his paintings. I instantly knew who she was and the tone of her stories.

Many thanks, too, to every person who has left their fingerprints on this work: my agent, Susan Cohen; Dorie Bailey, editorial manager at PPB; Caitlin Ek, marketing associate; Katelyn Keating, production manager; copy editors Margery Schwartz and Leilah Bernstein; book designers Susan Olinsky and Amy Inouye; and interns Julia Cooke and Julianne Johnson. Also appreciation goes to Dru Ann Love, Coleen Nakamura, Maria Kwong, and Debbie Mitsch for their input regarding book design. And I'm forever indebted to the Los Angeles Public Library, Los Angeles County Library, and Pasadena Public Library systems.

In hindsight, it's amazing that so many people and elements came into play to bring this Leilani Santiago mystery to you, the reader. I feel so humbled to have had this opportunity and have not taken it for granted. And, of course, thank you to our dog, Tulo, for keeping me company on those long days at the keyboard and my husband, Wes, for his patience as I carried stories of Hawai'i in my head.

About the Author

Naomi Hirahara is the Edgar Award–winning author of the Mas Arai mystery series. Also nominated for the Macavity and Anthony awards, the series includes the Edgar-nominated *Hiroshima Boy*, *Sayonara Slam*, *Strawberry Yellow*, *Blood Hina*, *Snakeskin Shamisen*, *Gasa-Gasa Girl*, and *Summer of the Big Bachi*. She is also the author of the Ellie Rush mystery series, as well as *1001 Cranes*, a novel for children. A graduate of Stanford University, Naomi has written many award-winning nonfiction books as well, about gardening and Japanese American history and culture, including *Life After Manzanar* and *Terminal Island: Lost Communities of Los Angeles Harbor*. She lives in Pasadena, California, with her husband. Learn more at naomihirahara.com.